"You must be a very good writer, because you've got an imagination on you..."

Jo laughed, partly because she was enjoying herself and partly because Thad had just voiced her thoughts.

Feeling good, Jo said, "Can I ask you something?"

"Anything."

"Last night..." She hesitated, but only for a millisecond. "Did you see me...inside the tub?"

He leaned close, his mouth right beside her ear. "You mean, did I see you naked?"

"Yes," she whispered, closing her eyes.

"Well, now, a gentleman would lie and say no." He took a deep breath, like he was breathing in her scent. "The question is..." His breath sifted the hair at the side of her head, making her shiver.

"Would you like me to be a gentleman...or not?"

Dear Reader,

I loved writing this book because it includes some of my favorite things (anyone else hear Julie Andrews singing "My Favorite Things"?) First of all, it's a Christmas book and I LOVE Christmas. However, I've never written a Christmas story before, and I wondered how I could capture its essence on the page.

For a start, I decided my office needed to smell like Christmas, so I loaded my diffuser with essential oils like cinnamon apple and sweet pumpkin pie, which helped but also left me feeling hungry all the time.

I played Christmas carols while I wrote, and plastered snowy images on my windows so that when I looked up from my computer, it seemed like a winter's day. Setting the book at the Silver Tree Guest Ranch in Western Montana, where there are snow-covered peaks and homey log houses, helped set the mood.

While this book includes traditional Christmas trimmings like mistletoe, homemade decorations, dogsledding, ice skating and stockings by the fire, I also wanted this story to be full of surprises. With this in mind, I put the heroine in an uncomfortable situation right off the bat. Think outdoor hot tub, a forgotten bathing suit and an overly helpful ranch hand with a penchant for disturbing the peace.

A Christmas Seduction is a story where family and strangers are thrown together, where there's secrets and intrigue all mixed up with eggnog, Christmas carols and, of course, hot, passionate cabin sex (yes, please!).

So grab your favorite Christmas beverage, curl up in front of the fire and enjoy!

Daire St. Denis

Daire St. Denis

A Christmas Seduction

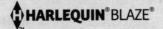

Recycling programs
for this product may
not exist in your area.

ISBN-13: 978-0-373-79926-8

A Christmas Seduction

Copyright © 2016 by Dara Lee Snow

Printed in U.S.A.

New York Times and *USA TODAY* bestselling author **Daire St. Denis** is an adventure seeker, an ancient history addict, a seasonal hermit and a wine lover. She calls the Canadian Rockies home and has the best job ever: writing smoking-hot contemporary romance where the pages are steeped in sensuality and there's always a dash of the unexpected. Find out more about Daire and subscribe to her newsletter at dairestdenis.com.

Books by Daire St. Denis

Harlequin Blaze

Sweet Seduction
Big Sky Seduction

For CJ Carmichael

1

A tip to travelers: always be prepared. No matter where you're going, carry an emergency kit with food, water, matches and other essentials…like a bathing suit.

Jo Duval

JO DUVAL'S PHONE BEEPED—again—but she ignored it. She was too busy navigating the lonely, snow-covered road from Half Moon Creek to the Silver Tree Guest Ranch. Growing up in Chicago, she was no stranger to winter driving, except for the fact that it was so blasted dark out here in the Montana boonies. Plus, she was all alone. It was just her and Michael Bublé, singing about chestnuts roasting on an open fire. No one knew where she was—her family, anyway—and her flight had been changed at the last minute, so she was arriving a day early. She'd called and left a message at the ranch, so presumably the hosts would be expecting her.

She hoped.

Despite the heat pouring out of the vents in the rented Jeep, she shivered.

What if she got lost on these back roads? Or stranded?

Her mind wandered to a scenario where she was driving a mountain pass—which she wasn't—and her Jeep skidded toward the guard rail, bumping against it so that she was face-to-face with the cliff and yawning abyss below. In her mind, she wrenched the steering wheel and at the last second, the Jeep swerved, spinning in the middle of the road and ending up in a snowbank on the other side. She'd have to spend the night in the vehicle. She mentally went through the contents of her handbag. What would serve in an emergency situation? She had two candy bars—okay, one and a half—a box of Tic Tacs and…

She reached for the can of soda in her cup holder, picked it up and gave it a gentle shake.

A sip of soda.

Things were not looking good. Did she have matches?

"I should really keep some, just in case," she muttered to herself.

Her phone beeped.

"I hear you. I hear you."

The light snow that had been falling suddenly intensified, so Jo turned on her wiper blades, though they didn't help much. The radio crackled, like it was snowing in there as well, and she turned it off.

"Sorry, Mr. Bublé."

Visibility was limited to about ten yards in front of the vehicle, and the way the snow came at the windshield was hypnotic, like she was in the cockpit of a spaceship driving at warp speed.

"Ground control to Major Tom," she sang softly.

She glanced at the clock.

It was only six thirty? How could that be? It felt so much later. The guy at the gas station in Half Moon Creek told her it was a thirty-minute drive out to the ranch. That was almost an hour ago. Felt like two. Leaning forward, she peered ahead, hoping to catch a glimpse of…something. A sign? A building?

Lights?

Yes, those were lights up ahead.

Thank God.

The headlights lit on a large sign—Silver Tree Guest Ranch. A few minutes after turning down the lane, Jo could make out the buildings: a barn, an enormous log home and other structures, all defined by white Christmas lights. With the snow accumulating on the trees and the buildings, and the shimmering lights peeking through the piles, it was like she'd walked onto a photo shoot for a Christmas card. She parked beneath a sign that read Visitor Parking, got out—phone in hand—and took a couple of pictures.

"Too dark," she muttered before making adjustments on the camera app in an attempt to capture the festive atmosphere of the place.

She held the phone in front of her and...heard barking.

Shit!

Three wolf-like creatures came bounding at her from the other side of the lodge. Jo dropped her phone and dove for the door of the Jeep. Her foot slipped and she careened off the side of the vehicle, landing flat on her butt in a pile of snow just as the beasts sprang at her, barking and yipping, about to maul her to death.

"Digger, down! Come."

With hands raised to protect her face, Jo felt the hot breath from the animals' snarling muzzles before they retreated, making whining sounds as they went.

"You okay?"

She lowered her hands to find a mountain of a man standing over her. He just went up and up. When he extended his hand, she flinched before realizing he was there to help.

"Come on. I got you."

Hesitantly, she took his hand, and in one swift movement, he hauled her to her feet. Unfortunately, her boots were not made for ice and her feet flew right out from beneath her again. With the man's hand still grasped tightly in hers, this time when she fell she pulled the stranger right down on top of her.

"Oomph." She sucked in a deep breath. The man's scent filled her lungs: cedar, smoke and something sweet. Licorice?

Practically nose to nose with him, she gazed into the stranger's eyes, noticing how they crinkled at the corners. Nice. For some reason her gaze dropped to his mouth. Full lips tilted up at the edges, and the longer she stared, the broader the smile grew.

She cleared her throat. "Would you mind getting off of me?"

"Apologies, miss." He chuckled.

She felt the rumbling of his laugh all the way through her winter parka. Jo did not share in his amusement. Embarrassment, on the other hand? Oh, yes. She felt that acutely.

The man eased off her and clambered to his feet. Once upright, he held his hand out for her again, making a show of bracing his legs this time. "Easy, now. I'd hate to crush you for a second time in less than five minutes of knowing you."

She batted his hand away. "I'm fine." Getting to her feet on her own was a necessity in circumstances such as this. She pushed herself up and dusted herself off, all the while eyeing the formidable canines who sat a few yards away, salivating and watching her with interest.

Like she was supper.

"You're a guest, I take it?"

"Yes." Never taking her eyes off the dogs, she edged toward the back of the Jeep.

"You're early."

"I am. I called ahead." She hazarded a quick glance at the man. "Are you Dillon Cross?"

"Nope. I'm Thad. The hand."

The hand? Was that a joke—at her expense—about the way he'd offered his hand to help her? She popped the back door of the Jeep and, after darting another glance at the pack of dogs, yanked her suitcase out. It toppled with a soft thud into the snow.

"Let me take that."

Before she could refuse, Thad had already stooped down and grabbed the luggage. When she didn't move because, quite frankly, the large, hairy beasts were blocking her path, he said, "Not a fan of dogs, I take it?"

"No."

He whistled, a low note ending on a higher pitch. "Go on." The dogs barked in response before the one in the middle ran off in the other direction, looking behind every few steps as if to make sure the other two followed.

"Thank you," she said, going back to the place where she'd fallen, intent on finding her dropped phone.

"You looking for this?"

The man had her phone and was holding it out for her. She reached for it, but his grip stayed firm.

"You'll never meet friendlier dogs. They're the welcome committee around here. Just wanted to say hello."

Barking, snarling and salivating was not exactly Jo's idea of a warm welcome, so she let Thad know what she thought by making a grunting sound at the back of her throat.

"To each their own," he muttered before trudging toward the lodge, suitcase in hand. However, once they made their way up onto the covered porch, he turned to her. "I've had Sue since she was a pup. She wouldn't hurt a flea, let alone a guest. The other two are her offspring. They're rambunctious, but gentle as spring lambs."

"If you say so." The stranger had an unmistakable Louisiana drawl, not what she expected to find in Montana. She supposed she should have anticipated dogs, however. Jo stomped her boots on the mat outside the door.

"If you'd like, I could introduce you to them…"

Thankfully the topic was dropped when the door swung open and a petite woman stood in the opening, a huge smile on her face and a Santa hat sitting at a jaunty angle on her head, covering red curls. "You must be Jolie! I'm Gloria Cross. Welcome to Silver Tree Ranch. We're so pleased to have you."

THAD SET JOLIE'S bag down in the entry of the ranch house. Four things tipped him off to her city-girl status. Her designer clothes, her designer bag, her ridiculous footwear and her fear of animals.

He nodded to Gloria while the new arrival removed her winter outerwear.

"I hope I'm not inconveniencing you by being early."

"No, not a problem." Gloria glanced at Thad. "Join us for supper? I made winter soup and biscuits."

"I do love your biscuits, Ms. Gloria," he said. "But I've got chores yet. I'll grab something in the bunkhouse."

"You sure?"

"Positive." He tipped his hat to Gloria and when the other woman—Jolie—straightened from removing her winter boots, which were not meant for winter, he tipped his hat to her, as well. As she stood there in her oversized sweater and tights, Thad could see she was tall: arms and legs from here to there. She reminded him of the fawn that got trapped on the sheer ice of the pond last winter: brown

hair, brown doe eyes with long lashes, long spindly legs…
no coordination.

The image was so striking he had to cover a chuckle
with a cough.

"Come by later if you feel like it," Gloria called as he
ducked back out. "Dillon's itching to break into the rum
and eggnog."

"Thank you, Ms. Gloria, but I'm saving my imbibing
for Tip's Eve."

The door shut behind him and he whistled for the dogs.
They'd been sitting by the side of the house waiting for
him, and he kneeled down in the snow to give all three a
proper head scratch. As far as he was concerned, there was
something wrong with a person who didn't like dogs. Not
that the canines didn't like this Jolie woman. It was a good
sign, because if the dogs didn't like someone…well then,
that meant there was *really* something wrong.

No matter. It wasn't the first time one of the guests had
been skittish around the animals. Even though the ranch
had been open for business for only a little over a year,
he'd seen it before. While Thad didn't understand an aver-
sion to dogs, he recognized that anyone who was booking
a stay over Christmas didn't have any other place to be.
This woman had arrived alone, which could only mean
one thing: she had no family to speak of.

Thad knew firsthand how lonely that could be over the
holidays. It'd been eleven years…

Hell, what was he doing, ruminating over the past? That
never did a man any good. Particularly him.

He stood and the biggest of the three dogs cozied up
to his legs, rubbing against him before placing his paws
on Thad's thigh.

He knew what was coming next.

"Don't you dare, Humper," he warned.

But the young dog didn't heed the warning. His tongue lolled out of his mouth and his eyes rolled back as he launched into the action that was his namesake.

AFTER A DELICIOUS DINNER of hearty chicken soup and warm biscuits, Jo sat at the desk in her room—the best guest room in the whole place, Gloria had said—typing notes into the file for *Travel America Magazine*. Thank God they had decent Wi-Fi, though Gloria had said they'd had to install a satellite because the service was so bad when she first moved here. Impossible to have a business these days without access to internet. Jolie arched her back and rolled her shoulders just as her phone beeped for what seemed like the millionth time. She should have turned off the ringer but she supposed she'd left it on as a sort of punishment.

"Fine," she grumbled, picking it up and quickly scrolling through the messages. Ten from her mother. Two from her father. All with the same message.

Call me.

Or...

Call your mother.

Leaning back in her chair, she dialed her mother's cell and waited.

"I've been trying to get hold of you all day. Why haven't you called me back?" she asked by way of a greeting.

"I'm..." Jo gazed about the large room. The log walls made the space feel warm and rustic, and they were complemented by Southwestern accents: rugs, pillows, throws. "On assignment," she finished absently.

"Well, I need to firm up the meal for the twenty-fifth. Your father wants halibut this year, so if you could bring a pilaf or risotto and a salad… Your brother is bringing the wine. We'll eat at two and then I'm on call at the hospital from eight to eight."

Jo squeezed her eyes shut. "I'm not—"

"Oh, and no gifts this year. We're donating to Oxfam in lieu."

"—coming."

Silence.

Finally, "Excuse me?"

Taking a couple of deep breaths first, Jo said, "I won't be there."

"Why not?" Her mother's tone was not disappointed or hurt. Just curious.

"I'm on assignment," she repeated. "So, I won't be in Chicago for Chris…for the twenty-fifth." As theirs was an atheist household, Jolie's parents did not approve of using the word *Christmas*. Instead they called it "the holiday," "the twenty-fifth"—anything but "Christmas."

It's disrespectful to celebrate a day that honors the birth of someone or something we don't believe in was the explanation she'd received when she was eight years old.

"Where are you?"

"I can't say."

"Why can't you say?"

Yeah, Jo. Why can't you say? "I'm investigating something." She surfed through news articles on the web, hovering over the link to one about a trial involving alleged members of an organized crime ring. Clicking on the article, she skimmed while her mind made up a tall tale to tell her mother. "It's a big story. Organized crime. If I can be the first to break it, my career will take off."

"You should talk to your brother. He's prosecuting a

case right now involving organized crime." Her mother's tone was emotionless, which made it impossible to determine if she was trying to be helpful or making an assumption that Jolie needed the assistance of her brother.

"Look, Mom, I've got to go." She paused. "Tell Dad I said hi."

"Of course."

"I'll miss you."

"Let me know how the story goes."

"Sure thing," Jo said, but her mother had already hung up.

She sat for a minute, staring blindly at her screen before finally snapping the laptop shut. What had compelled her to lie? Why hadn't she just told her mother she was spending the holidays with friends or that she wanted to know what it was like to *really* celebrate Christmas?

Sighing, Jo pushed herself to her feet and went to open the blinds that covered the French doors leading out onto the deck. It was the reason Gloria had said this was the best room—next to hers and Dillon's on the second floor, of course. This one had direct access to the deck and the brand-new hot tub.

She rolled her shoulders again, groaning because her neck and upper back were stiff and sore from the tension of driving through a blizzard at night. Falling flat on her ass probably didn't help either.

Relaxing in a hot tub would be wonderful. Too bad she hadn't thought to bring a swimsuit.

She unlatched the lock and pushed the sliding door open before stepping out onto the covered portion of the deck. Though she couldn't see past the edge because of the inky blackness and falling snow, from the pictures on the internet, she knew the view from here would be spectacular. She closed her eyes, envisioning the picturesque scene she would wake up to tomorrow: forests and fields with mountains in the distance. A pond out front, surrounded by snow-covered trees.

Idyllic.

Jo opened her eyes. The soft whirring of the hot tub's motor drew her close. She flipped the lid and steam rose up to greet her.

Go ahead and use it, if you'd like. Nothing like a hot soak on a snowy night, Gloria had said.

Jo trailed her fingers through the hot water. Oh, it would feel so good…

She glanced up at the house. The lights that should have been shining through the French doors and windows off the main floor had all been extinguished. Her hosts must have gone to bed.

She was the only one up. The only guest.

"Why not?" she whispered to herself, pulling her sweater over her head and dropping it on a nearby table. Next she pulled off her leggings and socks, followed by her underwear. She squealed softly when the cold air caressed her naked skin, and scurried up the steps of the tub. She stepped in gingerly while covering her bits before sinking beneath the water.

"Ahhh," she sighed, letting her head fall back against the headrest. "This is the life."

If her mother could see her now, she knew exactly what she'd say. *Hot tubs are breeding grounds for bacteria.*

She laughed softly to herself. Then her smile faded as she considered the lie she'd told. Why had she done it? It probably had something to do with the fact that her family thought her career choice was a waste of time.

You can't make a living as a writer, her father had chided when she'd told him she was taking creative writing at college.

So, she changed majors and went into journalism.

Unfortunately so far, even with a journalism degree, her father had been right. Since graduation, the only writing gigs she could get were for online publications—for pauper's pay—and freelance travel articles. Which paid only marginally better, and that wasn't saying much.

Jo was determined to prove her family wrong. All she had to do was break a big story—kind of like the lie she'd told her mother this evening—and she'd be taken seriously as a journalist. The problem was, she had no big story. No leads.

Nothing.

Jo turned her head. A control panel blinked to the left of her and she tested some of the buttons. The first one turned on music, a mellow jazz something or other. That was nice. She tried another button and the lights inside the tub came on.

A downward glance revealed her state of undress and she pressed the button once more, except instead of turning off, the lights simply changed color from blue to red. Another touch of the button and the lights turned green.

"Seriously?"

One more time and the internal lights flickered, strobe-light-style, as if there was a dance party going on in the tub. One she was not keen to take part in.

Before she could hit the button again, the sound of a dog barking froze her in place, her finger stuck in pressing position.

Glancing up, she gasped to find *the hand* standing on the far side of the tub, grinning. "Well, heya, miss. Something I can help you with?"

2

The best thing about traveling alone is you get to be the person you want to be because no one knows any different.

Jo Duval

THAD HAD SEEN the flashing lights as he made his way from the barn to the bunkhouse, and something had drawn him over. Had he known the dog hater would be naked—apparently she wasn't *all* arms and legs—he'd have steered clear.

Probably.

"Just press that button one more time and the lights will go off," he said as he backed up a step to give her some privacy. He could be a gentleman if he had to be.

The lights inside the tub went out and the woman became nothing more than a shadow surrounded by a cloud of fog. "Thanks. You can—"

"It's nice, isn't it?" Thad murmured to the hazy outline of the woman. "Ms. Gloria and Dillon just got the soaker last week. Haven't tried it out yet myself, but I installed it, so I know how it works."

"Right. Um, would you mind—"

"So, how long are you here for?" Thad asked, biting down on his lip to control his grin. He could be a gentleman, but he could also be a right jackass. Why he felt the need to torture this woman, he couldn't say exactly.

"Oh, um…eleven days." She cleared her throat. "I don't mean to be—"

"Right on into the New Year? That's a nice long stay." Thad was having a hard time containing his enjoyment as he pressed on. "Do you enjoy winter sports? Skiing, ice-skating? That sort of thing?"

"I'm sure they're fine, but—"

"Lots to do around here. I'm your man if you're interested." That sounded like a come-on, which was not his intention, but he couldn't seem to stop himself from tormenting this woman.

"Look, Mr… What did you say your name was again?"

"Thad. Thaddeus Knight, at your service."

"Mr. Knight. I'm all good. You can leave now."

"Of course. Didn't mean to disturb you, miss," he lied.

"You didn't disturb anything." Her voice was high. Nervous.

"Okay then. You enjoy your soak and I'll see you tomorrow."

"Mmm-hmm. Bye, now."

He glanced over his shoulder only when he hit the edge of the deck. Sound always traveled better at night, and he clearly heard the ornery woman swearing beneath her breath as he took his leave, the very mutts she scorned waiting for him at the bottom of the steps.

He shouldn't have done it, shouldn't have taunted her, particularly when he realized she was bathing in the raw. His grandmother would have said the devil possessed him, and that might be true. But he didn't think that was all there was to it. There was something about the woman, something that drew him, something he couldn't quite put his finger on.

JOLIE LAY SNUG under the covers, existing in that space between sleep and wakefulness. It was her preferred mode of waking every day because it was when her imagination took over, ungoverned by inhibitions and the critical internal editor who was her regular companion during the rest of the day—though so far, this morning had remained completely silent.

Perfect.

Jo revisited the scene in the hot tub, but this time she wasn't embarrassed by her state of undress. This time she was bold and flirty. This time she flaunted her nakedness, turning the lights on in the tub—to red—instead of turning them off.

"What did you say your name was?"

"Thaddeus Knight. At your service."

"You said you're a hand. What does that mean, exactly?"

"I could tell you, but showing you would be way more fun." His gaze swept over her body, his blue eyes dark with desire.

"Then you'd better show me."

"It'd be my pleasure."

He removed his hat and winter jacket—

It was one of those cowboy-style ones. They had a name, oilskin or something? She'd have to look it up later...

"Shh," she muttered to herself as her internal editor started to rouse. She willed herself to focus once more on the vivid scene playing out behind her closed lids.

"Close your eyes," he said in that deep Southern drawl.

She obliged him, then rested her head against the edge of the tub, feeling the submersion of his body by the way the water lapped higher up her chest.

"Give me your hand."

Languidly, she lifted her hand out of the tub and presented it to him.

"You have nice fingers. A nice hand."

"Thank you." She sighed with pleasure as he began to massage her palm. "So do you."

He did have nice hands. Big and strong—she remembered how they'd felt when he'd tried to help her up after she'd freaked out.

"Shh," she said aloud, working a little harder this time to slip back into her fantasy.

Thad worked the tender part of flesh between thumb and forefinger before sliding his hands up to her forearm, massaging as he went.

"You're very good at this."

"I'm good at a lot of things."

"I bet you are," she purred.

"Do you want me to show you?"

"Yes."

His hands moved up higher to her shoulders, pausing to massage before caressing her collarbones and then dipping down her chest to her breasts.

"Is this okay?"

"It's wonderful."

He fondled over and under before gently pinching a nipple.

She groaned.

"You're so beautiful. I wanted you from the moment I saw you."

Jolie's eyes popped open.

I wanted you from the moment I saw you?

Seriously?

Creating sexual fantasies featuring a virtual stranger as a sort of ranch gigolo? Ridiculous. How did she ever expect to make it as a serious journalist when she wiled away her spare time coming up with this sort of nonsense?

Jo sat up, threw off the quilts and swung her legs out of bed. She went to the French doors and drew back the blinds.

"Beautiful," she said matter-of-factly. The view was exactly like the panoramic shot on the webpage.

While she might not be an acclaimed journalist yet, she was still here to do a job, so she sat down, opened her laptop and called up her travel article. After tapping out a few awkward sentences and random ideas, she stared at the screen.

Screw it.

Going over to her bag, Jo took out her leather-bound journal, a gift from her father last year.

I know writers do everything on computer, but I thought you might like this. Or not. Here's the gift receipt if you decide to return it.

She hadn't returned it. It was the best gift her father had ever given her. Opening the journal up to her last entry, she reread what she'd written a couple of days ago and then began writing—longhand. She didn't even have to think; the words just poured out of her as she filled page after page, like she was merely the conduit for ideas coming from another realm.

The aroma of fresh coffee and bacon drew her out of the story and back to reality, her stomach growling.

After dressing, she joined her host in the dining room, where breakfast was already laid out.

"I hope you slept okay," Gloria said while she poured the coffee.

"Amazing."

"The rest of the guests arrive today. Festivities begin once everyone's here. We'll go out and cut a tree and then decorate it tonight while we celebrate Tip's Eve."

"Tip's Eve?" Jo was thankful to have something else to discuss.

"It's a tradition of Thad's, from his Catholic roots, I think. Anyway, it's a pre-Christmas party, always on the twenty-third. We thought it would be fun for the guests."

"Sounds like it." Jolie smiled as warmth infused her, starting at her core and radiating out to her extremities. The sensation had to do with the thought of celebrating any kind of Christmas tradition and had nothing to do with the mention of Thad's name.

Nothing whatsoever.

"How many guests do you expect?"

"Only five, including you. It's our first time opening up the ranch to guests over the holidays."

Jolie nodded and took a bite of omelet, which she'd drowned in ketchup.

"So," Gloria said, drawing out the one-syllable word as she sat opposite her. "You're a writer?"

"Journalist." Why did she correct her? She liked the title of writer.

"And you're doing an article about the ranch for *Travel America*?"

Jo looked up, nodding as she chewed.

"I hope you'll take into consideration the fact that we're still in the development stage…"

"Oh." Jo wiped her mouth with the cloth napkin. "This isn't a travel critique of the place or anything. I'm here to enjoy myself and then write about it. That's all."

"Okay." A blush crept up Gloria's neck and into her cheeks. "I'll be honest—I've been feeling a bit of pressure knowing you were coming. I just really want this ranch to take off, you know?"

"Please think of me as just another guest."

Gloria released a big sigh. "Right. Well, you let me know if there's anything you need. Anything at all. And if I can't help, then I'm sure Dillon would be happy to. Or Thad."

Jolie's throat felt funny.

"Well, speak of the devil."

The omelet in her stomach flipped over at the sound of boots approaching on the wooden floor. Head bowed toward her plate, she looked up through her lashes to see Dillon enter the room, still wearing a winter parka, his cheeks rosy from cold. Following close on his heels was Thad and another man Jo hadn't met yet.

"Morning, boys. How are things?"

"Good." Dillon kissed his wife, and Jo couldn't help watching as Gloria gently rested a hand on her husband's chest. Jo quickly averted her eyes. Unfortunately, they ended up landing to the right…which was where Mr. Thaddeus Knight was standing.

He winked.

"Thad tells me you tried out the hot tub last night," Dillon said.

Oh, good God.

"Mmm-hmm," Jolie intoned. What else had Thad said?

"It's good for a body. Helps you sleep."

"Sure does." Jo could not meet Dillon's gaze. Or anyone's, for that matter.

"Have you met Curtis?"

Thankful for the change of subject, Jo looked up and greeted the third man with a smile. Then the discussion turned to the estimated arrival times of the rest of the guests and all mention of the hot tub ceased as the men sat down to eat, Thad taking the seat right beside her.

"Morning, Ms. Jolie. You're looking well."

His words were drawn out, one syllable running into the next with weird inflections that seemed to mock, or could be suggestive. It was hard to tell with that Southern accent, which only served to remind Jolie of her early-morning fantasy session.

Could he tell what she was thinking?

"Thank you," she mumbled before stuffing a forkful of egg into her mouth.

Thad's right hand was within her line of sight, because it rested right beside her plate. She stared. His hand was exactly as she'd imagined it. Large and well formed, tanned—or maybe that was just his olive skin tone. His fingers were long and veins stood out on the back, like he actually had muscles in there.

Vivid images from her early-morning musings filtered through her mind. She glanced up. "You said you're a hand. What does that mean, exactly?"

"I could tell you, but showing you would be way more fun."

Déjà vu struck.

"Then you'd better show me," she said, as if reading from a preordained script.

"It would be my pleasure."

Chills ran up her spine, sifting through her hair and settling on the crown of her head as she stared into Thad's eyes. His dark blue eyes.

Cerulean, cobalt, indigo… Her writer's mind came up with a list of synonyms for *blue* while she got lost in the azure depths of his gaze.

An idea washed over her as she dove into that ocean of blue. What if she stopped being embarrassed about the fact that she'd been caught skinny-dipping? What if she embraced it…no, *flaunted* it, instead? What if Thad really was interested—like in her fantasy—and what if she welcomed it? What would it be like to be that person?

"What size are your feet?"

Hell, she could be anyone she wanted to be on this trip. No one knew her. No one would know the difference.

Thad snapped his fingers in front of her face. "Hello?"

"Huh?" Oh, God. He was talking to her and she was staring at him openmouthed. She gave her head a shake. "Sorry. I—"

"You were a long way off just now. Everything okay?"

"Yeah. Perfect." She smiled. "What did you say? Something about feet?"

"I asked you what size you are. Thought you could borrow some boots because if you're going to be traipsing around in the snow and ice, you need a better pair of footwear than the ones you drove up in."

"Oh…right. I'm size eight."

"Do you have a size eight she could borrow?" Thad asked Gloria.

"I'm sure I can find something."

"All right, then. You get suited up, miss, and meet me in the yard in ten."

WHILE THAD WAITED for Jolie to get dressed, a car drove up the lane toward the ranch. He squinted in the bright sun, made brighter by all the newly fallen snow. The car was one of those sporty deals, meant for city driving. Not for snowy country roads. Good thing whoever it was had arrived this morning instead of last night.

Once the car was parked, a man and a boy got out. The boy was probably about nine or ten years old, his hair stuck up at all angles, like it hadn't been combed in a good couple of days. His eyes were wide and uncertain as he took in the surroundings.

Thad started over, the dogs on his heels, but Humper couldn't contain his zealous nature and went bounding on ahead, straight at the kid.

"Humper!" He didn't want a repeat of last night.

Too late. Humper launched himself at the boy, toppling him into the fresh pile of snow. Thankfully the sounds the kid made were ones of laughter and not abject fear. Not like the soft whimpering notes that Jolie had been making last night.

A sudden image of Jolie lying naked beneath him, blinded him. She was making the very same noises as she had last night, only in his fantasy it was from pleasure, not fear.

Thad rubbed his eyes.

Where the hell had that thought come from?

Probably the result of watching that crazy dog. He whistled and Humper looked up, tongue lolling in ecstasy. That goddamn mutt's tongue was too big for his fat head. He ignored Thad, focused on the boy, who was standing upright again, and gave in to his basic urges.

Striding up to the dog, he pulled him off. "Sorry about that, kid. This dog's still young and trying to exert his dominance on anything that moves. Even some things that don't move."

"It's okay," the boy said. "He reminds me of Biscuit."

"You've got a dog, do you?"

The boy glanced at the man. "Well…we used to. He went to a farm. Right, Dad?"

"Right." The guy mussed the top of his son's head. His eyes were tired. Sad. There was a story there; Thad could see it plain as if the title of a book was written across the man's forehead.

"Would you like to meet the other two?" Sue and Digger sat obediently a few yards away.

"Yeah!"

A short whistle brought the other animals over and after a quick introduction, the kid was running around the yard with three ecstatic dogs chasing him while his father carried the bags inside.

Thad turned. He'd been aware of the woman's presence, as she came to stand behind him, before she'd even said a word. Why he sensed her like he did, he couldn't say. Was it her scent? That sweet, delicious smell of peppermint candy?

"Hi."

"Hiya, city slicker."

She grimaced at the name but then pointed at one of the animals that was chasing the kid around on the other side of the yard. "The dog's name is Humper?"

She continued to watch the chase and he took the opportunity to study her. She looked different by day. In the bright light, her brown hair had honey streaks running through it, and her big eyes were flecked with gold. Her mouth was wide, probably too wide, but he liked it, particularly when she smiled. In fact, he wanted to see one of those smiles right about now.

"He comes by it honestly," Thad explained when she met his gaze again. "Sue went out looking for a baby-daddy a year and a half ago. Must have been slim pickin's because, while these mutts are friendly, they aren't exactly the sharpest tools in the shed."

There it was. The smile he'd been going for. Too bad she went and covered it up with her mitten, because he was pretty sure her grin had turned into a laugh.

"What's so funny?"

She shrugged. "I just had this image…"

"Of?"

"Your dog, what's its name?"

"Sue."

"Yeah, of Sue looking over her shoulder in exasperation and telling her newfound baby-daddy, 'Stop talking, just do me.'"

Huh. City girl had a sense of humor. She'd even done a bit of a Southern drawl for Sue, which was adorable. He chuckled. "Yeah, well, instinct is a powerful thing and when 'the heat' hits, even a smart one like Sue will take whatever she can get."

She smiled.

Damn, she had a lovely mouth. The kind of mouth that was meant for kissing. His gaze dropped without warning and even though she was covered up with a winter coat, he easily recalled what was underneath. He shouldn't have spied. But he didn't regret it. Not one bit.

It took effort to lift his gaze again and unfortunately the broad smile he'd been enjoying was already gone, replaced by a wide-eyed look of fear.

3

When on vacation I always make a point of trying
new things. After all, isn't that what traveling is all
about?

Jo Duval

ONE SECOND SHE was feeling warm and flirty, and the next
the cold hand of dread wrapped itself firmly around her
throat. Squeezing.

The boy was running their way followed by the three
hounds from hell, nipping at his heels. It made no difference they had amusing names. The dogs were big, they
were loud and they had incredibly sharp teeth. Just then,
the boy's father called to him from the porch, telling him
to come inside. With a groan, the boy made his way to the
house, complaining the whole way, leaving the dogs with
no one to molest…except her.

Without thinking about what she was doing, Jo hid behind Thad, pressing herself right up against his back and
clutching his arms like they were life preservers. If she
could have crawled into his skin, she would have.

The sharp sound of Thad's whistle only made her clamp
on more fiercely, and while she was aware of him speaking, she could not make out the words.

Eventually, Thad took hold of her hands and got her

to release him as he eased her into the circle of his arms. "Hey. Hey," he said softly.

She opened her eyes.

"It's okay." He smiled down at her. "I sent them away."

Dammit. So much for her attempt to be someone different on this trip.

"You are seriously scared of dogs, aren't you?"

"You think?" She forced a laugh even though her fear was anything but funny.

"What happened to you?" He brushed a wisp of hair out of her face.

"I got bit." She tried to recall the incident, but it was vague. "I barely remember it because I was so young, but ever since I've been terrified of dogs. It's…incapacitating."

She looked up and realized—oh, shit—she was fully ensconced in Thad's big, strong arms, her mittened hand resting on his chest, an affectionate gesture, much like she'd witnessed between Gloria and Dillon an hour ago. While she may have invented a seductive scenario starring Thad this morning, he was a complete stranger, someone she'd known for less than twenty-four hours, and finding herself wrapped in his arms—while very nice—was a little *too* familiar.

She backed away from his embrace and he let her go.

"You interested in overcoming that fear?"

"Maybe. But…" She was about to say *not today* when he whistled, a short, sharp sound, and the older dog, who she assumed was Sue, ran over, her offspring following right behind. Though one stopped to sniff, nosing around in the snow before setting in to dig with a vengeance.

"And…that is Digger," he said wryly.

She remembered the name from last night. In the daylight, the animals were certainly friendlier looking. The one named Humper sat and stared with his tongue hanging out one side of his mouth. Digger, a mostly black dog with white tips on his ears, just kept digging, turning one way and then another, snow and dirt flying out from behind him.

The dog named Sue sat by her master's leg, gazing up at him with adoration before turning that gaze on Jo. She could see the intelligence in the dog's face, her eyes rimmed with white fur, like she was wearing a mask, almost appearing human as she blinked at Jolie.

Okay, maybe they weren't so bad.

"Put your hand out."

"Huh?"

Thad took her arm, pulled off her mitten and arranged her hand palm up. "Let Sue sniff you."

When the dog approached, Jo's automatic response was to pull away, but Thad held her hand in place. The dog sniffed her before resting its chin in her upturned palm.

"Oh."

Thad knelt down beside the dog, still holding Jo's hand. With his other hand, he scratched the top of the dog's head. "She likes it, right behind the ears. Like this." He gazed up at her, his blue eyes brighter in the sun. "Give it a try."

I can do this. I can.

Hesitating for only a second, Jo let her hand be guided by Thad's until she was touching the soft fur on the top of the dog's head. She buried her fingers into it, scratching gently.

"Now you've got it."

The dog shifted to lean against her leg and Jo jumped. She pulled her hand away, not because she was scared but because the dog's movement startled her.

She looked at her hand. "Oh, my God," she whispered. "I touched her. Did you see that? I touched a dog."

"Did more than touch her. You gave her a real good scratch."

"I did, didn't I?" On some level, Jo knew how ridiculous it must seem, that she was overjoyed by the simple act of petting a dog. But to her this was huge, and the result was that she felt invincible. Superhuman. Like she could do anything, anything at all.

So she did. When Thad stood, she turned toward him, put one mittened hand on his cheek while her bare hand gripped the front of his jacket. Then she went up on tiptoe and kissed him full on the mouth.

HER LIPS WERE cold but that didn't stop Thad from enjoying City Slicker's mouth slanting generously over his. She started to pull away, but he stopped her by threading his fingers through her hair—silky soft—and holding her close. He intended to warm up those lips, taste the inside of her mouth, get her to taste a little more of him if she was willing.

Yep. She was willing.

He'd suspected that full mouth of hers was made for kissing, and he was right. While the woman might be apprehensive when it came to animals, her kiss indicated that she'd be anything but wary when it came to messing around beneath the sheets. An image of just such a scenario had Thad adjusting her head so he could kiss her even more deeply.

Suddenly she gasped, sucking the air right out of his lungs and into hers as she pulled away, staring up at him like she was just seeing him for the first time.

"Oh, my God. I kissed you."

"Yes, you did." The hand on his chest pushed but Thad held on, not letting her get away just yet.

"I shouldn't have done that."

"Why not?"

She tilted her head to one side. Blinked. Opened her

mouth to speak and then closed it. Finally she said, "I'm not..." then paused. After another couple of rapid blinks, a small smile touched the edges of her wide mouth. "You know what? I'm *not* sorry."

"No?" He felt his lips turn up, mirroring hers. "Good. 'Cause I'm not either."

"I'm glad." She gazed into his eyes, half smiling, half frowning, as if she couldn't quite make up her mind about the situation.

"I wouldn't complain if you wanted to take another shot—"

"Thad?"

Shit. He turned to see Curtis walking across the yard. "You gonna come help finish chores or what?"

"Yep. I'm on my way." He squeezed Jolie's hands. "Chores call. You coming?"

Her features still waffled between a smile and a frown. She settled on the frown. "Uh...you know what? I'd better go do some work myself."

SITTING AT THE DESK in her room, Jolie tried to work on her article for *Travel America*, except every time she started typing, she found herself caught up in an instant replay of kissing Thad. She should be embarrassed...except she wasn't. At all. How could she be when Thad was such a good kisser? The way he held on to the back of her head, tilting her the way he wanted her, holding her close? The way his lips were both soft and firm, lulling and commanding all at once?

Divine.

The way he'd used his tongue on the inside of her lips, tracing them, tasting her?

Heavenly.

The way he tasted of black licorice?

Delicious.

She ran her thumb over her lips, letting her lids flutter closed in recollection, playing the kiss over one more time, adding a few embellishments along the way. Like Thad's hand dropping to her ass, his head dipping low in order to whisper naughty things in her ear.

Glancing at the top of her screen, she read through some of her previous entries. *Be the person you've always wanted to be... Try new things.*

"What are you going to do, Jo?" she asked herself. Was she just going to write those things for the sake of the article? Or was she going to live them?

Pounding the desk, she muttered, "Dammit. I'm going to *live* them!"

A second later, a knock sounded at her door and when Jo called for whoever it was to come in—what if it was Thad?—the door opened and Gloria peered inside. "We're heading out to find a tree. Do you want to come?"

"I wouldn't miss it."

She grabbed her jacket and followed Gloria to the porch, where the rest of the guests had congregated. Their hostess introduced everyone: there was the father-and-son duo, Simon and Zak, and a young couple, Kaylee and Evan.

"We just got married last month," Kaylee explained, beaming with happiness. "This is our first Christmas together."

After congratulations, Gloria said, "I hope we can make your stay a memorable one." Then she clapped her gloved hands. "And we'll start by finding the best damn Christmas tree there is. Dillon says the nicest ones grow up on that ridge." She pointed to a spot that looked an awfully long way away. "As long as everyone's game, we thought we'd ride up there."

"As in, horses?" Jo blurted amidst the sounds of excitement from the rest of the guests.

"Yes. Is there anyone who hasn't ridden before?"

Jo raised her hand. Other than Zak, she was the only one, and her resolve to be the daring, adventurous Jo she'd always wanted to be slipped.

"Why doesn't Zak ride with me for his first time," Dillon offered.

While Zak complained that he wanted to ride his own horse, his father nodded, saying he thought it was a good idea.

"Evan and I can ride together," Kaylee piped up, winking at her new husband.

"What about you, Jo?" Gloria asked. "Do you want your own horse, or would you prefer to ride with someone?"

"She can ride with me." Thad was leaning against the rail, watching her carefully. His gaze created a little tickle at the back of her throat.

"Okay," she replied thickly. "I'll ride with Thad."

"That's settled, then." Gloria pointed toward the barn. "We'd better get going. The sun sets early this time of year."

Jolie followed the rest of the group toward the barn, feeling light-headed. It wasn't nerves exactly; it was...excitement? Excitement and anxiety all mixed up together?

With a dash of arousal?

She could still feel the effects of Thad's gaze, which was warm, probing...kind of like his tongue.

Once inside the barn, her mixed feelings only intensified. Horses were beautiful animals, but they were also big and scary, which both thrilled and terrified her. Then she considered Thad. There was something seriously hot about watching a man do something he was really good at, and he was clearly good with horses. Good with animals in general.

People, too.

Within no time at all, Thad, Curtis and Dillon had saddled up six horses, and everyone who knew what they were doing mounted. Once on top of his horse, Dillon leaned down, instructing Zak to take his hand so Dillon could pull him up in front of him. Evan did the same with Kaylee.

It was just Jo left.

"Take my hand," a deep voice said from above her.

"I'm a little bigger than the others," she replied, feeling insecure all of a sudden.

"I got you."

"You said that last night."

"I don't make the same mistake twice." He grinned. "Now put your right foot in the stirrup to give yourself a boost."

She did as she was told and, true to his word, Thad pulled her right up onto the horse. It was awkward getting her left leg over to the other side, but thanks to her bi-weekly yoga routine, she managed it without any mishaps.

"There now, you all right?" Thad asked, the words tickling the inside of her ear.

"I'm fine," she said, wriggling in the saddle. "But this can't be very comfortable for you."

"On the contrary. I find it *very* comfortable."

"Oh!" Jo wasn't sure if her exclamation was the result of Thad's big body snugging right up to hers—his thighs on either side of her legs, his chest pressed against her back, his arms wrapped loosely around her waist—or because the horse had started moving. She leaned back into him and the horse stopped.

"As much as I enjoy you leaning against me," he whispered roughly, "you need to sit up straight for the horse to move."

"Oh…okay." She sat up and the horse started walking again, following the others out into the yard. It was such a strange sensation, sitting up so high on the back of an animal, swaying side to side with the horse's undulating gait. Completely unnatural…yet kind of cool, too.

"You okay?" Thad asked softly.

His deep, melodic voice sent shivers into the pit of her stomach. "I'm okay."

"You let me know if you're not."

"I will."

The other horses moved off ahead of them in single file and they brought up the rear. Slowly.

"You're tense."

"Am I?"

"Yep, and the horse senses it."

"I don't know how to *not* be tense." She tried to turn in the saddle to face him, felt off balance and swiveled back around, grappling for the knobby thing on the saddle.

He tightened his arms around her and she immediately felt better. She closed her eyes and breathed in deeply, his scent reminding her of their kiss.

"Talking is a good way to keep the mind occupied, so you don't overthink things."

"Okay."

When she didn't say anything—because quite frankly she was still thinking about that kiss—Thad said, "Want me to start?"

"Sure."

"Where you from?"

Before she could answer, he said, "No. Let me guess… Chicago."

"How'd you know?"

"Well, you're clearly from the city and you sound like Gloria when you talk." He flashed a grin. "She's originally from Chicago, too."

"And you're from Louisiana. Am I right?"

"Good ear."

"What brought you all the way out here?"

He was quiet for a few moments. "Work, mostly. What about you? What brings you to a guest ranch in Montana?"

"Same. Work." This time when Jolie had the urge to turn her head, she controlled it. "I'm writing an article about the ranch for a magazine."

"You're a writer, huh?"

"Yes." She liked being called a writer.

She leaned back and the horse stopped.

"Miss Jolie," Thad murmured. "You need to sit up."

"Sorry."

"So…" he said. "You've never touched a dog, never ridden a horse. Now look at you. This day is full of firsts for you."

"That's my goal for this trip. To try new things, every day."

"It's a good motto."

The other horses were getting farther and farther ahead. Jolie didn't mind. She liked feeling as though it was just her and Thad on this ride, cozied up together, getting to know one another…

Suddenly an unpleasant thought intruded. "I suppose this is nothing new for you."

"Riding? It's part of the job description."

"No. I mean, *taking care* of the guests."

His arms stiffened around her. "And when you say 'taking care of,' what exactly do you mean?"

"You know…flirting with the guests."

"Are you asking if I go around kissing guests on a regular basis?"

She shrugged. "Maybe."

He transferred the reins to his left hand and gently caressed her thigh with his right. "I do not go around kissing guests. And may I remind you who kissed who first?"

She covered his wandering hand. Not because she wanted him to stop; only because she couldn't think straight when he was doing that. "I was excited. It was meant to be a little peck."

"That wasn't a peck."

"You're the one who made it into something more," she insisted, smiling as she recalled the kiss. Again.

"Is that the story you're going with?"

"Mmm-hmm." Jolie marveled at how easy it was to banter with this man. Along with her lack of skills with animals, repartee was another art she had not even come close to perfecting in her twenty-eight years.

"You must be a very good writer, because you've got quite an imagination on you."

She laughed, partly because she was enjoying herself and also because Thad had just voiced her thoughts. She'd never had that happen before.

Feeling good, Jo said, "Can I ask you something?"

"Anything."

"Last night…" She hesitated, but only for a millisecond. "Did you see me…inside the tub?"

He leaned close, his mouth right beside her ear. "You mean did I see you naked?"

"Yes," she whispered, closing her eyes.

"Well now, a gentleman would lie and say no." He took a deep breath, like he was inhaling her scent. "The question is—" his breath sifted the hair at the side of her head, making her shiver "—would you like me to be a gentleman...or not?"

4

One of the highlights of a trip is to experience new customs. Believe it or not, this is possible even in your own country.

Jo Duval

WOULD SHE LIKE HIM to be a gentleman or not? Oh, good Lord. What kind of question was that?

The best kind.

Jolie wriggled in the saddle. For some reason, her movement made Thad grunt and shift in response. She only heard the faint sound because he was still so close, his body fused to her back, his face hovering just above her left shoulder.

She cleared her throat. "I'd like the truth."

He turned, threading his fingers through hers. Such an intimate gesture.

Leaning down even closer—his lips within touching distance of her ear—he whispered, "I think you know the answer."

"I do." She wondered if he heard her, because the words were more air than sound.

"Are you shocked?"

She shook her head.

He let her hand go in order to capture her chin and turn her face so their gazes could meet. His eyes reflected the bright sun, giving his rugged features an almost other-worldly quality. "I apologize for the inappropriateness."

The lines bracketing his eyes deepened, telling Jo he was not sorry in the least.

She wet her lips and his gaze dropped to her mouth. Her stomach swirled in anticipation of something. Another kiss, maybe?

Oh, yes, please!

Thad's lids slid half-closed and Jolie lifted her chin in invitation.

Waiting.

She licked her lips again.

Nothing happened.

"Uh, Ms. Jolie?" Thad coughed or laughed—it was hard to tell with her eyes shut.

She opened them. The horse had stopped moving. She turned in the saddle. All the other horses were circled around, facing them. Curious glances and secretive smiles from the guests and hosts made Jolie's cheeks heat. She sat up straight, removing contact between herself and Thad.

Dillon cleared his throat. "Plenty of good trees to choose from here." He dismounted. "We're looking for one about nine feet tall." He reached up high, showing everyone about how big the tree should be. "Anything catch your eye?"

"How about that one?" Zak called, pointing to a large tree just to Dillon's right.

Dillon circled around the tree, checking out the branches and the height. "I think this one is pretty near perfect. Any objections?"

"Looks good to me."

"I like it."

"It's lovely."

"Thad? You've got the ax?"

"Of course I do. You know me—always prepared."

Why did just the sound of the man's voice send shivers down her spine? And then when Thad took her hands gently in his and gave her the reins? Shivers coursed over her shoulders and ran the length of her arms.

"You hold tight to these, Ms. Jolie, while I go help with the tree." As he leaned forward to dismount, he rasped, "And don't think I'm not going to finish what was started back there on the trail. I mean to kiss you like you've never been kissed before."

Jolie's doe-eyed gaze and wide parted mouth stole the air right out of Thad's lungs. Lord, the woman was a looker. He hadn't seen it so much last night; he'd been too focused on her fear of the dogs. Then there was the tub, and he'd been too intent on teasing her to really notice her looks. Her nudity? Oh, hell yes, he'd noticed that just fine.

But now, with her cheeks pink from the air—or was that a blush?—and her brown-gold eyes shining in the light, she was something else. How he'd wanted to taste those lips again. Particularly when she was apparently so willing, her chin tilted up, waiting, expectant, so close…so sweet.

Someone tugged on his sleeve.

Gloria stood there, smiling up at him, though something in her clear blue gaze told him she was none too pleased. She spoke in a harsh whisper through her fake smile. "What the hell do you think you're doing?"

"Why, Ms. Gloria." He held up the ax. "I was about to help that husband of yours chop down this fine tree."

The phony smile that spread across her face was in direct proportion to the degree her brows drew together in displeasure. "That's not what I mean," she whisper-yelled. Gloria flicked her gaze in Jolie's direction. "Don't you dare screw this up for us."

"Well now, I would assure you I wouldn't except that I don't know what you're talking about."

Gloria's chin came up in frustration and Thad had a hard time keeping his grin in check.

She tugged on his arm, pulling him in a direction away from the circle of horses. "Come take a look at this tree," she said, loud enough for everyone to hear. "Maybe we'll chop two. One for the foyer and one for the great room."

Once they were out of hearing distance, Gloria punched Thad on the arm.

"Ouch." He feigned injury.

She poked him in the chest. "Stop screwing with our guest."

"I'm not screwing with her."

"No, but you'd like to." She threw her hands up in the air. "Men. Can't you keep it in your pants, just once?"

Thad gave her a second to rant about the unruliness of male sexual desire.

"She's a guest and you work here. It would be totally inappropriate."

"Kinda like sleeping with your boss?" That stopped her long enough for him to continue. "So you're saying I can't take her up to the Doghouse?"

Gloria's eyes went wide at the mention of the old homestead that sat up on the hill, the place she and Dillon had used multiple times as a rendezvous point for sexual trysts when she'd first come out to Montana. When she'd been in Dillon's employ.

"A little hypocritical of you, don't you think?"

She crossed her arms over her chest and pursed her lips. Then her features softened as she turned her head to gaze up the hill at where the place stood. "I just…" She sighed. "It's really important Jolie write a favorable article about the place. It could make or break us."

Thad propped his arm across Gloria's shoulders and gave her a reassuring squeeze. For as much as he loved tormenting this woman, he cared deeply for her and for Dillon. Plus, he needed the job, and this place was the perfect cover for him.

"So, what do you want me to do?"

"Stay away from her."

"What if she can't stay away from me?"

She elbowed him in the ribs. "Tell her it's part of the rules. You can make her feel comfortable, special, but stay out of her bed and no kissing."

"You're no fun at all."

"I know you, Thaddeus Knight. The longest relationship you've had lasted all of twelve hours." She glanced back toward the group. "This writer, she doesn't seem like the one-night stand type. You know?"

Damn. Maybe she was right. Thad wasn't a relationship kind of guy. His life didn't allow it. His gaze followed Gloria's. "Okay," he said finally. "I'll keep my hands to myself."

"Good." She looked him up and down. "And everything else, too."

JOLIE HAD NEVER decorated a Christmas tree—not a real one, anyway. There was the fake minitree she'd bought for her tiny apartment a couple years ago, with all the cute little decorations to go with it. But a real live tree?

Never.

Even before hanging decorations, the big tree took her breath away, twinkling with multicolored lights and bringing its fresh pine scent indoors. She helped herself to a glass of mulled wine and stood back from the group, watching the flurry of activity with a warmth that spread from her tummy out to her extremities. After riding back to the ranch with Gloria—so that Thad could haul the tree—she'd decided to head to Half Moon Creek to pick up a couple of things.

New boots? Check.

A bathing suit? Check, check.

Some gifts for her hosts and the guests? Check, check, check.

Plus she had a special surprise tucked away in a florist's box in her room. She went to retrieve it now, glancing over her shoulder to see if Thad might follow, feeling giddy after her second glass of spiced wine.

Thad didn't follow. What did she expect? He was working and she wasn't the only guest. She retrieved the box and presented it to Gloria.

"What is it?"

"Open it."

Gloria opened it and gasped. "Real mistletoe?" She grinned. "That's so thoughtful."

"Half Moon has the sweetest little florist shop, and the girl was so helpful. She…" Thad joined them at that moment and her sentence trailed off as she gazed up at him. More specifically, at the way his shirt stretched across his broad shoulders and opened at his throat, giving her a glimpse of the strong cords of his neck.

She'd like to sink her teeth into them.

"Do you want me to hang that?" His lips twitched and Jo's gaze slid to his lips, imagining his mouth moving closer and closer to hers.

"Sure, that'd be great," Gloria answered. Then she turned to the rest of the room and clapped her hands. "Okay, everyone, let's get decorating. There are plenty in the boxes or you can come on over to the dining table and help make some."

The last time Jolie had made a Christmas ornament was

in grade school—when the whole class made them—and she eagerly joined Gloria at the large dining room table where there were bowls of multicolored candies, cookie cutters and molds of different sizes all laid out on cookie sheets.

Kaylee joined them. "Oh! Christmas candy ornaments. I saw this on Pinterest."

Gloria explained how they were going to melt the cut rock Christmas candies into beautiful, tasty ornaments. Jo half listened to the instructions as she snuck glances at Thad out of her peripheral vision. He was hanging the mistletoe from the door frame that separated the large dining room from the great room.

While Gloria was busy explaining how to make the ornaments, Jolie was busy imagining a scenario under the mistletoe.

"So, we'll just spray some oil on the inside of these molds and then place the candies loosely inside..."

She was *accidentally* standing beneath the mistletoe when Thad walked by. He looked up. She looked up. Their gazes met.

"We'll pop them in the oven so the candies melt together..."

He bent down to kiss her and...shit! He'd caught her watching. Grinning, he stalked toward her, and Jo's pulse fluttered in her veins as he closed the distance between them.

"Once they've cooled, we'll tie ribbons to hang them and this is how they'll look." Gloria held up some samples of ornaments that looked like mini stained glass windows.

"Don't mind if I do, Ms. Gloria." Thad plucked a decoration out of her hand and stuck the candy in his mouth.

"Thaddeus Knight. That is an ornament for the tree. It is *not* for you."

He bit down on the hard candy, snapping it in two, and offered the other half to Jolie. "It was all Ms. Jolie's fault." He winked.

She smiled up at him. It was impossible not to beam in delight when Thad was around. Except his grin froze when Gloria caught his eye. She scowled at him. It was only when she met Jo's gaze that her smile reappeared.

Apparently she was very serious about these ornaments.

"Why don't you go give Dillon a hand with the garland." Gloria waved toward the other room.

"I'm thinking this candy operation looks like more fun."

"Thad…" There was a warning note in Gloria's voice.

What was that about?

Whatever it was, Thad ignored it. He propped his arm across Jo's shoulders and said in a conspiratorial voice, "Now, ladies, did y'all know that the barn out there is haunted?"

"Haunted?" Kaylee asked, intrigued.

"Oh, yeah." He winked at Gloria. "You remember, Ms. Gloria? There was that one time I was heading for the barn, needing to get something from the tack room at the back…" Thad scratched his jaw, all serious now. "This must have been a year ago now? Maybe a year and a half? Anyway, there was this awful strange sound coming from that room."

"What kind of sounds?" Jo leaned closer.

"Scratching. Panting. A woman's scream…or sigh. It was hard to tell."

"No way," Kaylee said, eyes wide.

"Yes, ma'am. I been careful going in there ever since. Never know what a body will find." His grin was pure wickedness as he smiled at Gloria.

"Thank you for that, Thaddeus," Gloria said, giving him a shove toward the great room. When she returned to the table, her cheeks and neck were flushed bright red. "Now, let's make some ornaments."

Jo had just started filling up her molds with candies when Gloria came to stand beside her. "I apologize for Thad."

"What do you mean?"

She crinkled her nose. "He's a flirt."

"No need to apologize for that."

"Just be careful."

"Careful?"

"I…" Gloria frowned. "You know, even though he's worked here awhile, we still don't know all that much about him."

"What are you saying? Don't you trust him?"

She opened her mouth to reply, but Dillon appeared at her side at that moment, carrying an open box of ornaments. "Hey, Red. Curtis found these in the Quonset. They must be from Kenny's family." He picked out an ornament wrapped in tissue paper and passed it to Gloria, who unwrapped a pretty colored glass ball.

"Oh, this one's beautiful."

"What should we do with them?"

"Let me sort through them. I'm sure we can use some."

Jo frowned after Gloria's retreating back. Why would Gloria warn her about Thad? Was there something dark and dangerous in his past? The very idea got Jolie's creative juices flowing and she considered all sorts of possibilities.

If Gloria's intention had been to warn her off Thad, it was having the opposite effect, because all Jo could think about was ways to seduce him.

She smiled as a vivid image of how she could get him into her bed came to mind.

This was going to be the best Christmas *ever*.

THE FITTED RED turtleneck and black skirt Jolie wore suited her, probably because they fit so well. The turtleneck reminded him of all her lovely curves; the skirt looked feminine and showed off her long, shapely legs. She was a sight, that was for sure, her eyes shining brightly in the candlelight as everyone sat around the fireplace in the great room. Now that the tree was done, they ate and drank and chatted as if they'd all known each other forever. It'd been a long time since Thad had spent the holidays with other folks. Not that he didn't like people. He liked them just fine; he just had to be careful of strangers.

Funny how they'd all just met, but there was something about the holidays that made people more open, made this setting more familial.

More intimate.

He glanced Jo's way and caught her watching him. Her cheeks flushed. Was that due to him or was it the combination of the fire and mulled wine?

Maybe both. Either way, he liked it.

He had wanted to heed Ms. Gloria's warnings, but there was something about this woman that he couldn't seem to shake. He just had to be near her. His fingers twitched with wanting to touch; his nostrils flared with wanting to sniff—did she always smell like peppermint?—and he found himself constantly wetting his lips, longing for another taste.

He hadn't meant to tease Ms. Gloria about overhearing her and Dillon in the tack room that time, but he couldn't resist. Kind of like he couldn't seem to help himself around Jolie.

Of course he should stay away from her. He never got too close to anyone, couldn't afford to, but...

He met her eyes again. Beautiful doe eyes. Sweet. Innocent. Yet he knew from the kiss out in the yard that she had a fire burning inside of her. That and her innocent passion was an intoxicating combination.

"So," Jo said, holding his gaze. "What is Tip's Eve?"

"Well now, it comes from some of my Cajun, Catholic roots."

"You're Cajun?"

"I'm a little of this and a little of that." He changed the subject from his family back to the tradition. "Catholics are all about abstinence followed by overindulging." He lifted his rum and eggnog. "It's the pre-Christmas party for all of us who can't wait for the twenty-fourth."

"Cheers to that," Zak's dad said.

"Cheers." Zak ran around the room clinking his glass of punch with all of the adults' glasses.

It'd been a long time since Thad had been around a kid. Something about that brought back memories, stuff he hadn't thought about in years. "Now, Zak," Thad said, "have you heard of *Père Noël*?"

Sitting back down on the rug in front of the fire, Zak shook his head, eyes wide. "What's a pear Noel?"

"*Père Noël* is French for 'Papa Christmas.' You know about Santa Claus, right?"

His head bobbed up and down real quick.

"Well, lots of kids are curious how Santa can get all around the world in one night, leaving presents for all those kids. You ever wonder 'bout that?"

"Yeah, I wonder that sometimes." Zak glanced at his dad. "But, he's magic, right?"

"Oh, yeah. Most definitely. But that's not all." Thad leaned down, as if he was talking only to the kid, but out of the corner of his eye, he watched Jolie, aware of her more than anyone else in the room. "I'll tell you a secret about how Santa does it, but you've got to promise not to tell anyone else."

Zak scooted closer, coming to sit right down at his feet. "I promise," he whispered excitedly.

"Okay, well...the secret is, there's more than one Santa."

"What?"

Thad turned to Jolie because she was the one who'd uttered the question, not Zak.

"Sorry, keep going." She waved at him to continue.

"It's true. There's the one that lives up north, there's one that lives in Sweden, there's one from Russia, a couple from Africa. Probably a few down in Asia—there's lots of kids there. And there's one that lives in the swamps of Louisiana, and his name is Papa Noel."

"Really?"

"Mmm-hmm. You think about it, not every place is cold. A sled doesn't work where there's no snow. Papa Noel? He doesn't have reindeer and a sleigh, he's got a pirogue—you know what a pirogue is?"

The kid shook his head.

"It's a flat-bottomed boat that skims nice and light over the swamps." Thad glided one hand over the other to illustrate. "Now...instead of reindeer, what do you figure pulls Papa Noel's pirogue?"

"I don't know," the kid said.

Thad glanced up. Jolie's eyes were as wide as the boy's. Her gorgeous mouth parted a bit.

"Gators."

"No." Again, this came from Jolie, not the kid.

"Oh, yeah," Kaylee, the young newlywed said. "I had a storybook about Papa Noel when I was a kid."

"Well now, if it's written down in a book, that must make it truth."

The boy nodded as if that made perfect sense, and Thad went on to explain how in Louisiana they set up huge bonfires on Christmas Eve to light the way for Papa Noel because it could be so dark at that time of year.

"Can we light a bonfire?" The boy looked at Dillon excitedly. "Can we? So Santa doesn't get lost?"

Thad didn't wait for Dillon to answer. Pointing to the big fireplace, he said, "We don't need bonfires. We got a fireplace to let him know where we're at."

His story led to others in the group swapping their own, and while Dillon talked, Thad got up to refill his glass with eggnog, smiling as he ladled. What was it about this year that felt so different? It'd been almost twelve years since he'd left NOLA. Since Katrina and everything that came before. But this was the first Christmas he actually felt like he belonged somewhere.

It was nice.

A soft step followed by the scent of peppermint alerted Thad to her presence.

"That was quite the story," she said, her voice husky and low.

Thad shut his eyes before answering because he already knew why this holiday felt different.

Jolie.

5

Want to spice up your holiday? Try a holiday fling.
                                                    Jo Duval

THAD TURNED TO find Jolie gazing up at him, her eyes sparkling in the candlelight.

"You like Christmas stories, do you?"

"Who doesn't?" She pointed at his glass. "Is that eggnog?"

"Yep."

"Homemade?"

"Of course."

She eyed his glass.

"Did you want some?"

"Oh, no…it's just that I've never tried it."

"Seriously, woman. Where've you been at? A nunnery?" He held his glass out to her.

Without hesitation, she took it from his hands and sipped.

"Ooh. That is good." She took another sip. "Mmm. Filling but delicious."

After a third sip, Thad drawled, "Do you want to keep that one?"

With a laugh she handed it back. "No. I'll stick to my mulled wine." She picked up the mug she'd set on the table and backed up a step, then two.

"Can I refill your mug for you?"

"Sure."

He took it from her hands, their fingers touching briefly, hers long, slim and delicate.

Nice.

He ladled steaming wine inside and handed it back, wanting to touch again.

"Thank you." Smiling, she shuffled back another step, her gaze flicking to the rafters.

Thad's eyes followed and he realized that she'd positioned herself under the mistletoe. On purpose? He'd just have to see about that, now, wouldn't he?

Leaning against the door frame, he pretended like he wasn't onto her. That damn devil that lived beneath his skin rubbed its hands together at the thought of tormenting the woman. Just a little.

"So, Ms. Jolie, where y'at?"

"Excuse me?"

"Just wondering how you're doing. Did you have a good day?"

"Oh…yes. It was lovely." Her gaze went skyward then came back down.

"You sore at all?" His gaze slid low and lingered because she had the nicest legs.

She coughed. "Uh…not yet. Should I be?"

Thad shrugged. "Dunno." He crossed his arms at his chest and moved one boot over the other, as if setting himself up for a nice long standoff. Sha. Why did he enjoy torturing this woman so much? "Depends what kind of shape you're in, I guess."

She shifted her feet. "I'm in decent shape."

Thad concurred as he allowed his gaze to take her in, nice and slow. "Then you should be just fine." An understatement. The woman was more than fine, particularly

right now, because there was something sinful sparkling
in those pretty brown eyes of hers.

Pushing himself from the wall, he moved closer.

Her chin lifted and her gaze went to the mistletoe again.
Yep, she knew exactly what was what.

"You need anything else?" he asked huskily, noticing
how her full lips parted. Then that sweet, sweet tongue
made an appearance, passing over her lips, making them
nice and moist.

"I, uh…"

"I'm here for whatever you need. Just name it."

Her chest rose and fell. Then she wet her lips again.

Her mouth was his undoing. He leaned down. "Tell me."

She made no bones about the mistletoe this time. Looking straight at him, she blinked and then tilted her head up.

Damn Gloria and her warning. Thad was only so strong,
and when a woman like Jolie Duval wanted him to kiss
her, who was he to deny her?

Pretending he hadn't noticed the mistletoe until this
very moment, Thad said, "Well, look at that. Seems as if
you've been caught under the mistletoe, now, doesn't it?"

"Seems that way."

"You know that means I'm going to have to kiss you."

"I suppose those are the rules."

"Yes," he said softly, reaching for her chin. "They are."
He tilted her face up and placed what he figured was a
gentlemanly kiss on her soft, succulent lips. In fact, her
lips were so tasty, he licked—that was less than gentlemanly—and damn if she didn't taste like peppermint. A
sweet, wet, candy-cane kiss.

Oh, it would be so easy to get carried away—her mouth
was so generous and giving, her body so warm and pli-
able. How the hell had she ended up pressed against his

chest, her soft womanly curves fitting perfectly within the circle of his arms?

Laughter from the great room brought Thad back to his senses and he ended the kiss, though he really didn't want to. Oh, no. Here's what he wanted…to take her hand and lead her down the hall to her room. Once inside, he'd peel her clothes off like the cellophane on a candy cane and lick all that peppermint sweetness from her skin. Teasing and tormenting her until she screamed.

"Thanks, that was nice." She stroked his cheek, smiling secretively, as if she could see his X-rated thoughts dancing like sugar plums inside of his head.

Jolie extricated herself from his embrace and walked off, swishing her hips and whistling softly, like it was she, not he, who would be doing the teasing and tormenting.

Jo LOOKED AT the line that she'd written the day before "Have a holiday fling…" and backspaced over it. Then she typed it again and erased it once more. *Have a holiday fling?* What kind of advice was that? This was supposed to be a family vacation destination, not a hedonism resort.

Ugh.

She spent the next few minutes detailing the authentic Christmas ambience of the ranch, the celebration of Tip's Eve—making decorations, eating and drinking, laughing and telling stories—and included some pictures she'd taken. There. That was better. She smiled, thinking about how much she'd enjoyed last night.

Have a holiday fling.

She'd never had a fling.

Wait a second…

Jolie rubbed her cheek. There was her lit professor at college. He'd invited her over to his place to help him grade papers; he'd wined and dined her, seduced her. Hmm.

Upon reflection, that was *probably* a fling, though she'd thought it was more—naive girl.

Then there was her brother's friend Kyle. They'd hooked up a couple of times and—yep, same thing—she'd imagined there was more to it.

What was wrong with her? Hopelessly romantic? Incredibly naive?

Not this time. This time it was going to be different because she knew *exactly* what she was getting into. A fling. Plain and simple. Nothing else. No expectations, no emotional attachment.

Just a superhot holiday fling.

Jo shut her eyes, replaying the scene under the mistletoe. She knew one thing for sure: she wanted another kiss. No, she wanted more than that, because she'd never felt more alive and more desirable than when Thad had lifted her chin and kissed her.

Jo opened her eyes and reached for her notebook, the words practically falling off her fingertips as her pencil flew over the page. The ideas came so quickly she could barely keep up. Not ideas—it was more like watching a movie inside her head. A supersexy movie. Time lost all meaning when she was like this, and Jo was surprised to find it was ten thirty when she finally closed her journal.

Picking up the pretty paper itinerary that Gloria had given her the first night, instructing her to take part in as many or as few activities as she liked, Jo ran a finger down the list for the day. Eleven o'clock was ice-skating on the pond.

Ice-skating was one thing Jo knew how to do. Too bad she hadn't brought her own skates. She'd taken figure skating lessons as a kid and though she was no superstar, she had a few skills. Was it wrong that she wanted to show off a little bit for Thad? Let him know she wasn't inept when it came to *all* physical activities?

A blinding image of some of the *physical activities* she'd written about made her pause.

"C'mon, Jo," she muttered to herself. "You can either sit here and daydream about it, or you can get out there and make it happen." Her tummy tightened. Jolie Duval was about to have herself a holiday fling.

DRESSED IN TWO pairs of leggings, a wool sweater, a cap, mitts and parka, Jolie made her way down to the section of the pond that had been cleared for skating. Before she could go through the boxes of used skates to find a pair that fit her, Thad ambled over. She knew it was him by the shadow he cast and by her body's automatic response to his.

"Do you like history, Ms. Jolie?" What was it about his deep Louisiana drawl that got under her skin—in a good and tingly way?

"Sure," Jo said, looking up from where she crouched, her heart in her throat.

"Ever seen a ghost town?"

"No." She stood, her legs feeling awfully strange for some reason.

"What about a dogsled? You ever gone for a ride on one?" Thad came closer, so close she could smell his freshly showered skin, and she noticed his hair was damp.

"Uh…no," Jo replied slowly. An image of the man in the shower filtered through her consciousness.

"You interested?"

The shower suddenly included her making a guest appearance. It was so clear she could practically smell the soap. The two of them. Together. Naked. Wet…

"Ms. Jolie? Everything okay?"

"Yes," Jo said, barely seeing the real Thad because the imaginary one in her head was so…naked.

"Good. I've got lunch all packed. We can eat when we get there."

Wait. *What?* Jo frowned, watching Thad's retreating back. What had she just agreed to?

Thad was walking toward some sled, where the three hounds from hell were tethered. Oh, God no. Jo jogged to catch up. "Um…when I said yes…"

Thad stopped and turned.

She licked her lips and his gaze dropped to her mouth, which made speaking difficult. "What I meant was…" Her words trailed off because suddenly Thad was naked again—still soapy—and she was itching to touch him.

Strong hands covered hers and Jo realized—too late—that she'd pressed her mittened hands against his oilskin jacket.

"You're not backing out, are you?"

Jo shook her head.

"Good." Keeping hold of her hand, he tugged her toward the sled. "Let's go."

She was amazed at how easy it was to get over the fact that she was in such close proximity to dogs. Maybe because they were busy pulling the sled and weren't paying any attention to her. Or—more likely—it was because she was snuggled up in a blanket, drinking homemade hot chocolate from a thermos while Thad drove the sled.

He talked the entire time. Story after story after story. Most about this place, the people who lived here, the history, who owned which ranch, how many cattle. It shouldn't have been interesting, but there was something about the way Thad told a story—the timbre of his voice, maybe? The cadence?—that kept her spellbound. Of course, the man could read to her from the phone book and she'd probably be enthralled.

They traveled for more than an hour, over fields and across a frozen lake to a logging road that led to something out of an Old West movie. Broken-down carriages, dilapidated structures with wooden facades worn into a smooth gray color from time and the elements.

"This is it," Thad said as he drove the sled down what would have been the old main street. "This is Silverton."

"Why doesn't anyone live here?" she asked, taking photos with her phone's camera as they moved slowly up the street.

"A couple reasons. Silver prices dropped, the mine shut down, the railroad pulled up its tracks." Thad pointed to the building they were just passing. On the facade in faded letters was Silverton Station.

"And everyone just up and left?"

"I imagine a few stayed for a while. But then there was a fire. No reason to rebuild. Most went to the cities to start over." He drove the sled up to a building with a newly painted sign that read Silverton Hotel.

"It seems so odd."

"There are little towns like this all over the place." He helped her to her feet and then went to untether the dogs. As soon as they were free, all three took the opportunity to roll around in the snow.

Somehow the hounds didn't seem quite so hellish as they wriggled around on their backs, legs akimbo, covering themselves in snow. Like three little kids.

Huh.

Kind of cute. Well, that might be a stretch, but at least they weren't quite as scary.

Backing up so she could get a better picture of the building, Jolie said, "Why does this sign look new?" Upon closer inspection, a number of the places looked like they'd been refurbished, with freshly painted signs: Greely's Mercantile, Northwestern Bank, Smithson's Saddle and Tack.

"Half Moon Historic Society has done some work out here. They open to tourists in the summer but shut it down in winter because the road's impassable." He squinted. "I prefer it this way."

"Yeah. Me, too." Jolie wandered to the big boarded up window and tried to peek through one of the cracks.

"You want a tour or lunch first?"

"Lunch then tour."

They spent the next half hour sitting on the stoop of the hotel, eating leftover soup from thermoses and devouring bacon, lettuce and tomato sandwiches. Jo had enjoyed the soup the first night, but for some reason it tasted even better now. Was it the fresh air or the company?

She glanced up to catch Thad watching her.

"You like your food, don't you?"

She shrugged. "I'm normally a junk food junkie. But I'll take this any day of the week."

"I like a woman who likes…" He didn't finish, as if he didn't want to go there.

Too bad, because Jolie wanted him to. She wanted to know more about the kind of woman Thad liked because she highly doubted it was a woman like her. Plain, uncoordinated, scared of dogs…

She straightened her back. But that wasn't her, not on this trip, anyway. She scooted closer to him, so that their knees were touching. He glanced down, noticing the contact, a small smile lifting one side of his mouth.

"You know, during the gold and silver rush, there were almost ten thousand people who lived here." He indicated the empty other side of the street. "They've only restored a fraction of what was here."

"Seems so…sad," Jolie said.

"You don't find it creepy?"

"No, I love it." She took a last bite of sandwich, balled up the paper it'd been wrapped in and tucked it in the bag. Pushing herself to her feet, she went to go peek between the shutters of the old building next door. The inside was dark but she could make out shadowy shapes of furniture.

She wandered down to the next building. Thad was only a few steps behind, watching her. "Places like this have so many stories," she said as she dusted the snow off a bench that sat in front of what was once the barber shop—based on the painted pole—wishing she'd thought to bring her journal. She closed her eyes. "I can hear the ghosts."

"You talk to ghosts, do you?"

"Maybe." She grinned, eyes still shut. Tilting her head, listening, as if she really was communing with the spirits.

The bench creaked and Jo felt Thad's big body sit down beside her. "Tell me, what do the ghosts say?" The words were soft and his breath brushed her skin, making her shiver.

Angling her head to the other side, she tapped her lips. "Hmm." Then, turning toward the man sitting next to her, she opened her eyes and said, "They say this is the perfect place to hide a body."

6

Always make sure you are wearing the appropriate clothing for any outing. While designer boots might look cute, they are completely impractical in the mountains.

Jo Duval

THAD CHUCKLED AT her comment, making a sexy rumbling sound deep in his chest. Those startling blue eyes of his gazed into hers before dropping to her mouth. His stare made Jolie rub her lips together, wetting them in the process. Another deep sound from Thad precipitated a tightening in her abdomen until breathing became difficult. The direct result?

Her chest heaved.

Thad's eyes followed.

He reached for a stray wisp of hair that fluttered across her face and she sucked in a ragged breath; she'd forgotten to breathe again. When he rubbed the strand between his fingertips before tenderly tucking it inside her woolen hat, she let out the breath she'd been holding. While still gazing up into his face, Jo removed a mitten and reached for him. Now that he'd touched her, her fingers needed reciprocation.

Lightly, she traced a line from high up on his cheekbone down to the line of his jaw, loving the scratch of whiskers in between. Such a strong face. Such nice, chiseled lips. She loved how his mouth parted as her fingers danced across their fullness.

"Ms. Jolie?"

"Mmm?"

Thad captured her hand in his big warm one. His voice was deep and rough when he asked, "What are you doing now?"

"What does it feel like I'm doing?"

"Tempting me." A small smile played at the corners of his mouth.

Jolie extricated her hand from his and ran her thumb over his mouth again. "Good."

He shut his eyes and sighed, which Jolie took as permission to keep exploring his face.

"Look," he said softly, opening his eyes. "I don't know if this is such a good—"

"Why not?" she interrupted, running the backs of her knuckles along his jawline.

Thad blinked, his face hardening into cold stone. "Because I'm not the settling-down type."

"Neither am I." How easy the words came to her. Whether she believed them or not was another matter.

His lips curled. "Is that so?"

"Yep." She drew her fingers down the strong cords of his neck, imagining how muscular his chest must be. Dying to find out.

"So, what is it that you want from me, then?"

"I think you know."

"Hmm."

Shifting her gaze to his eyes, she said, "What do you want from me?"

Something flashed across Thad's rugged features, and Jolie stopped because it looked like pain. He drew his gaze away, staring up at the sky. "There's the thing I want and then there's the thing that's appropriate—"

Oh, for God's sake, she'd had enough. With her mittened hand, she grasped the collar of Thad's jacket, tugged him close and kissed the warning right out of his mouth.

For a millisecond his cold lips stiffened under hers and a blast of doubt shot through her, making her pause. But that's all it was, a millisecond, because Thad made another one of those deep groaning sounds that came from the very base of his chest, rumbling deliciously around in his rib cage so that she could feel the vibration of it. He wrapped a hand around the back of her neck and pulled her to him, kissing her like he meant it, warming up her lips until she parted for him, exploring her mouth like it was wonderfully mysterious, delicious and exciting.

Jolie tore off her remaining mitten and worked her bare hands up under Thad's jacket, pulling his shirttails out of his jeans so that she could feel skin. Nice, warm, masculine skin. His abs contracted beneath her cold fingertips and he sucked in a breath.

"Sorry," she whispered against his mouth, not feeling sorry at all.

He pressed her hands to his sides. "Don't be." He nibbled her lip. "Feel free to warm yourself up on any old part of me."

"Really?" She tilted her head back to meet his gaze. Biting down on her bottom lip, she popped the button on his jeans, watching for a reaction.

Thad's eyes rolled back. "You trying to kill me now?"

"The ghosts did say it was a good place to hide a body."

Thad's chuckle was half groan, half laugh, and when Jo went to ease his zipper down—good Lord, the man was aroused—it practically unzipped itself.

"Jo-lie…"

She loved the sound of her name drawn out over a groan. Loved how it tasted, moving from his mouth into hers. While their tongues battled over who owned it, Thad unzipped her parka and worked his hands up under her sweater. She gasped at the sensation of cold hands against the warm skin of her tummy. She moaned when he worked them up higher, sliding up her sides to her breasts, squeezing over her bra first before dipping inside the cups.

His fingers lightly pinched one nipple then the other and she arched into him, throwing her head back to gasp at the delightful sensation. Thad took advantage of her exposed throat, leaning down to kiss beneath her jaw, as he pushed the cups of her bra down to better access her flesh.

"You are something," he whispered against her throat before sucking on tender skin.

"Thad…"

She loved his rough touch. Loved how he played with her nipples while nibbling on her jaw and neck. Needing to be closer, she sat up and straddled his thighs. Holding on to his face, she kissed him hard as she ground herself against him.

Suddenly the dogs started barking—she'd completely forgotten about them—and she jumped, mashing her mouth against Thad's teeth.

"Ow." She pulled back.

"Dammit." Thad frowned and blotted her lip, showing her the drop of blood against his thumb. "You okay?"

With a hand to her mouth, Jo nodded. She was okay. More than okay. Fat lip aside, she felt better than she had in a long time.

Taking hold of her hips, Thad maneuvered Jolie to the side so that he could stand. He zipped up his jeans and whistled for the dogs to be quiet. After Jo finished adjusting her bra beneath her sweater, Thad held out a hand, much like he'd done that first night, and said, "We best get back."

Unlike that first night, Jo took Thad's hand and allowed him to pull her up, needing to touch him as much as possible. Because of her height, she was often awkward around men. But with Thad? For some reason with him things were different. Maybe it was because he was a tall man himself, or perhaps it was the way he looked at her with a bold and sinful smile. Maybe it was the way he said her name in that delicious Southern accent. Whatever the reason, she felt like a desirable woman when she was with him, and she'd take a fat lip any day if it meant feeling this way.

DESPITE THE COLD, Thad still felt aroused. Even after the hour-long sled ride back to the ranch. His body responded to Jolie like he'd just hit puberty and she was the woman who starred in every damn one of his wet dreams. It was ridiculous.

He blamed her mouth.

Yep. The whole ride home, he'd fantasized about that mouth of hers. Remembering how good it felt to kiss her. Imagining how good it'd feel to be naked with her and have her slithering down his body, licking and kissing as she went. Visualizing how smokin' hot it'd be if she were to wrap those pretty lips around him and suck him into that big, beautiful mouth.

Fuck.

The yips from the dogs intensified as the sled rounded the barn and the bunkhouse came into view. Though it was only late afternoon, the sun was already beginning to set and the air had grown much colder. He stopped the sled and removed the dogs' harnesses and turned to Jolie. She was still sitting, covered by the blanket, her face white, her lips blue.

Shit! The woman was frozen.

"Hey. You okay?"

She nodded and tried to smile but her lips didn't make it very far. Thad chucked off the blanket and scooped Jolie up into his arms, lifting her and carrying her to the bunk-house a few yards away. He knew things were serious when she didn't fight him but instead nestled right into him.

Propping her on his knee, he elbowed the door open and carried her through into his side of the building, setting her on the sofa right beside the wood-burning stove and covering her with a couple of big throws he kept on the couch.

"I don't know what happened…" Her words were slow and slurred. "I think I fell asleep there for a bit. I feel funny."

"You're a little hypothermic, hon." Thad opened the cast-iron door and set the kindling inside before lighting it with a match and blowing a flame into existence. "Let me just get this fire going and then I'll come warm you up." Once the tinder caught, he added a couple small pieces of wood, muttering for them to hurry up and catch because he could hear Jolie's teeth chattering now. Though chattering teeth were better than the alternative. As much as Thad wanted to see Jolie naked again, if she started taking her clothes off now, that would be a sign of severe hypothermia, where the body gets all messed up and people feel hot when they're really, really cold.

He blew into the fire some more until the dry wood burst into flames. Then he added a bunch of larger pieces of wood, adjusted the flue and closed the door so that the stove could heat up.

Ripping off his parka, Thad sat beside Jolie, pulled her onto his lap and wrapped his arms around her.

"I don't think I've ever felt so cold," she stammered.

"I'm sorry about that, Jolie. I really am."

Her whole body tensed and shivered inside his embrace. Then she turned her head a little. "How come you're not cold?"

"Because I was standing and moving around. Plus, I'm used to working outside all year long. My blood's grown thick, living up here." It was true; he didn't feel the cold like he used to when he first moved north. But that didn't quite tell the whole story. He wasn't about to divulge that it was dirty thoughts about *her* that had kept him warm. More than warm.

She twitched some more, a couple little shivers followed by one big shudder, and Thad said, "Honey, I'm going to take off this parka of yours. It's insulating the cold instead of letting in the warmth. Okay?"

She nodded and Thad adjusted her on his lap so he could unzip her jacket. So different from when he'd unzipped it earlier in the day, itching to get his hands on her. Now he just wanted to take care of her and make sure she was warm and safe.

Once her parka was off, he removed his shirt and instructed her to do the same so that they were skin to skin. "Put your hands under my arms."

She did and he swore.

"Sorry," she mumbled.

"Don't be. I'm the one who turned you into a damn icicle."

He cuddled her on his lap and in his arms until the cabin became a sauna from the pile of wood he'd loaded into the stove. He held her until well after the shudders stopped and the temperature of her hands matched the temperature of his body.

It was Jolie who moved first, drawing her arms out

from under his. Slowly. She didn't move away; she left her hands lying lightly on his chest. He couldn't help but admire how beautiful her hands were: long, slim fingers gently twining the dark hair between his pecs.

"You're very strong."

Thad didn't answer.

"No one's ever picked me up like that." She lifted her eyes to his, a hint of vulnerability in their beautiful brown depths. "Thank you."

He nodded. For some reason, his voice didn't want to work. Could be because her hands were moving again. Exploring. Softly circling his nipples and spreading out over his pecs and up, the tips of her fingers circling the purple scar on his left shoulder.

"What's this?"

"A scar." He wasn't about to tell her where he got it. Or how.

"Looks like a gunshot wound."

"Naw," Thad answered quickly, his mind searching for an alternative story. "Got punctured by a branch when I was out on a ride a while back."

"That must have hurt."

"It wasn't too bad," he lied. If she only knew. Thank God the bullet had passed right through, because he hadn't dared to go to a doc to get patched up properly.

She delicately circled the scar a couple more times before exploring lower, trailing down the middle of his chest to his abdomen. She ran a finger along one line of muscle and then another. "I don't think I've ever been with a man who was so strong."

Was that what she thought this was? Him being a dick, tricking her into taking off her clothes, just to get with her? "Jolie. This isn't a come-on. Stripping down was the fastest way—"

She put a finger to his lips.

"Shh… I know exactly what you did for me." She reached around behind her back and unclasped her bra. "And I know exactly how I want to thank you."

JOLIE BARELY RECOGNIZED HERSELF. Who was this bold, brazen woman who had no qualms about stripping in a virtual stranger's cabin? Whatever teeny doubt she had about her actions vanished the second her bra dropped and Thad looked at her. His gaze wasn't lascivious; it was something else. The way he slowly drew in a breath. The way his mouth stayed firm but his nostrils flared. The way his lids grew heavy and his gaze liquid. It was like he was awestruck or something.

It also didn't hurt when he whispered, "My God. You're beautiful."

Though she was warm now, his hand on her was warmer. She lifted her chest up into his palm as he cupped beneath her breast and ran a rough thumb across her nipple. When she shivered this time it was not because of cold but out of pure pleasure, and when he leaned down and sucked a nipple into his warm mouth, circling with his tongue, she cried out.

With a groan, Thad pulled away. She wanted to demand *Why the hell did you stop?* But then Thad was bending down and picking her up again, and this time she got to witness the effect of the wonderful maneuver on the play of muscles across his bare chest and down his arms. She ran her hand along his bicep, marveling at the strength evident from the bulge in his muscles as he carried her.

His bedroom was only a few steps away. Though it was dark, she could tell it was a small room because the bed was a step inside the door. He set her down and then reached for a light attached to the wall above the bed. The room was bathed in a golden glow. Jolie didn't spend much time checking out the small space; she was too focused on Thad and the way he was gazing down at where she was propped on her elbows, her chest bare.

She decided to take advantage of the position and lay back on the bed so she could touch herself.

"Whatever you do, don't stop."

She smiled, gnawing on her lower lip. "I won't, as long as you take off your jeans." Oh. She loved being bossy with this big man.

Apparently he liked it, too, because his lips turned up on one side in a seductive smile. "I'll take off my jeans if you take off your tights."

Pinching her nipple and arching her back—on purpose—she said, "You first."

"You drive a hard bargain, miss." His hands lingered on his belt buckle, not moving, and he seemed content to just stand there and watch her.

"Do you need help?" she asked, sliding closer to the edge of the bed where he stood.

"Naw. Just enjoying the view."

The belt opened and his fly popped. He was standing so close—within reaching distance—that Jolie was able to run her hand up the inside of his thigh. She could feel his strong, muscular legs beneath the denim, which was a turn-on but not as much as watching Thad slowly unzip his fly and then move back so he could push his jeans down and step out of them. When he stood, dressed only in his boxer shorts, she gasped from the glorious sight of him.

Gorgeous. The man was gorgeous.

She needed to touch.

But when she went to reach for him again, he stopped her.

"A deal's a deal." He pointed to her tights. "Off."

He didn't need to ask twice. Jolie lifted her ass off the bed and pushed the elastic waistband down over her hips, then brought her knees up and wriggled in an act she'd hoped would look provocative.

Dammit.

She'd forgotten she was wearing two pairs of leggings, and her feet got stuck as she twisted and kicked to get them free. Thad had to come to her rescue, pulling the tights off her legs, taking one big woolen sock with them and leaving the other behind.

Totally not the sexy, seductive look she was going for.

She sat up to remove it, but Thad pushed her gently back down. "Allow me."

If someone had asked her whether she thought taking someone's sock off could be hot, she would have said no.

And she would have been wrong.

Because the way Thad did it was seductive as hell. Jolie had no idea her feet were erogenous, but when Thad sat on the bed, her feet in his lap, his hand caressing her calf before rolling the sock down and pulling it off, it felt like he was stripping the most intimate part of her. When he took turns massaging her insteps, Jolie propped herself on her elbows to watch, her blood pumping and her breaths coming in short little pants as if he was touching her between her legs, not her feet.

"You like that?"

"Mmm."

Never taking his eyes from hers, he lifted a foot and kissed the top. Then, setting her foot aside, he caressed up higher, from calf to knees to thigh. "You've got the prettiest legs."

She sighed.

"Those tights you wear show them off. Tempting me to do things I shouldn't."

Jolie was incapable of forming sentences, particularly when Thad's hands reached up higher, stroking her hips, caressing and massaging; the feeling was even better than it'd been with her feet.

"I can't lie to you." He stretched out beside her. "I saw you that night in the tub. All of you." He played with the elastic around her panties. "Except this part."

Jolie lifted her hips off the bed in encouragement, but Thad chose to ignore her invitation.

Instead he ran his hand up the side of her ribs to her chest, drawing delicate lines around her breasts. "Is it wrong that I've been thinking about getting you naked ever since?"

Jolie shook her head. How could it be wrong when she'd been thinking the very same thing? Crazy, sexy, inappropriate thoughts about Thad. She'd even written them down, which was ludicrous. The idea that he'd shared her thoughts and that now they were acting on their secret desires was nothing short of miraculous.

His hands were gentle as he explored her body, up over her breasts to her shoulder, holding lightly to her neck as his thumb traced her jaw and lips. When he came close again, she opened her mouth and touched his thumb with her tongue. He groaned but didn't do anything about it except keep caressing her.

"Thad?"

"Yeah, baby?"

"I'm not fragile."

"Huh?"

"You don't have to be so…careful with me."

He took a slow breath, gritting his teeth, nostrils flaring. "You don't know what you're saying."

"Oh, yes, I do."

He shut his eyes for a second. What did he see back

there? Jolie could only guess, but when he opened again, there was something in the depths. Something dark and irreverent.

She liked dark and irreverent.

"Tell me what you want," he rasped.

Could she do it? Could she be honest with him?

She moistened her lips. Maybe the old Jolie wouldn't have had the guts, but this new Jolie? She did. "I want you to take me, Thad. Hard."

7

While on holiday, I rarely regret the things I do, and more often regret the things I don't do.

Jo Duval

LYING ON HER BACK, gazing up at Thad in the soft light, Jolie wondered if she'd gone too far. Asked for too much.

"Sha, Jolie…"

Wrapping her arms around his neck, she pulled herself up close and nibbled the edge of his jaw. "Please."

"Damn, woman."

He threaded his fingers through her hair and tugged, pulling her head back so her neck was exposed. He licked a cord along her neck and then held it gently between his teeth.

"Oh," she sighed, giving him more of her neck to do with as he wished.

He moved his mouth to her ear, licking and sucking, tasting the inner shell, tilting her head to give him better access. "You like it hard, huh?"

"And fast." She trailed her hands down his chest and paused for a millisecond at the waistband of his shorts, then she wriggled her fingers underneath.

Wow.

How was it possible to be so aroused? Deliciously, magnificently aroused? She wrapped her fingers around him and squeezed.

He groaned, removed her hand from his shorts and then rolled on top of her. Taking hold of both wrists, he pressed her questing hands into the mattress beside her head.

She loved it.

Parting her thighs, Jolie made room for him, arching upward just as he ground down into her. So good.

So, so good.

"Do you have any idea how sexy you are?" He bit the lobe of her ear and then moved lower to suck the skin of her neck.

Jolie had never felt sexy. Not until this trip. Not until she'd met this man. But now? Now she felt more than sexy. She felt wanton and provocative, and the feeling was exhilarating.

Still holding her wrists above her head, Thad transferred both to one hand and slid his other down the inside of her arm to her side, passing over her breast lightly en route to her throat and jaw. He rubbed his thumb back and forth across her lips and she parted, drawing him inside.

"Damn this mouth," he ground out, taking his thumb away so he could kiss her. Thoroughly. Licking the seam of her lips, then inside, sucking on her tongue when she went to meet him and plunging past to explore.

So good.

Needing to touch, she fought against the hold he had on her, but he held her firm, keeping her captive.

Why did she love it so much? She had no idea, but she had to show him, so she wrapped her legs around his waist, opening herself to him, needing him closer, needing as much contact with this man as possible.

"Jolie...?"

"Yes." Whatever he was asking, the answer was yes.

He leaned across her to the small bedside table, slid the drawer open and reached inside. He pulled out a plastic square and rolled off her. "Don't you dare move," he commanded.

She didn't budge; she was too taken with watching. He sat on the edge of the bed, pulled off his shorts and rolled the condom over his length. Jolie had a moment when it hit her—what she was doing and who she was doing it with—but then Thad was moving toward her, fitting his fingers beneath the elastic of her panties and sliding them down her legs until she forgot about second-guessing herself. Instead, she gave herself over to existing completely in the here and now. The sensation of her silky panties sliding off her feet, the heat that spread across her chest and down, pooling between her legs as Thad touched her for the first time.

"Beautiful."

His voice had a reverent quality to it that stole her breath. Or was it the sight of him hovering above her, big and masculine, sexy and maybe even a little fierce?

"Thad?"

He moved lower, kissing her hip and her belly. When she wriggled, he held her hips down. "Don't move."

Those two words sent prickles of arousal skittering across her skin.

"Open your legs."

He was being bossy now and Jolie reveled in it. Wanted it. She let her knees fall open and cool air tickled her heated flesh.

"You are as pretty here as you are everywhere else." Thad petted her, softly playing with her clit before sliding his fingers past her pussy lips, dipping just the tips into her warmth. "Oh, baby, you are wet."

Jolie moaned, lifting her hips, urging Thad to explore

her more thoroughly, to plunge deeper. He was being so gentle right now—which was lovely—but she wanted more. Needed more.

He moved in between her parted legs, drawing her knees up and bending them so that she was completely open, completely exposed. "I bet you taste sweet, too."

He rubbed his cheek along her inner thigh, stubble abrading the sensitive skin there, and Jolie groaned. She shut her eyes and arched, overcome by the sensation of Thad's hot breath on her most intimate place. When he flicked her clit with his tongue, her hips bucked against the firm hold he had on her.

"Open your eyes, honey. I want you to watch."

It took effort to open because what he was doing felt so damn good. Licking and sucking, using his tongue to penetrate. Jolie could hardly stand it. But when she finally managed to force her lids open to the sight of him lying between her thighs, his dark hair brushing her belly, his mouth moving back and forth, Jolie lost it.

Orgasm came hard and fast and she grappled for his shoulders, needing him to stop, needing him to keep going.

Thad sat up so that he could finger her while she came, pressing down on her clit with his thumb, magnifying her orgasm in a way that was wonderful and new. Just when the pulses were about to abate, he leaned in again and sucked, nice and hard, and Jolie shuddered with one final, massive aftershock.

Before she fully touched down again, he crawled up on top of her, kissing her breasts, her neck, her lips.

"Is this too much?" he asked as he fit himself between her thighs, the head of his cock pressed firmly between her damp folds.

"No." She wrapped her arms around him, feeling both spent yet still in need of more. "It's not too much at all."

With a groan he adjusted his hips and thrust.

Oh!

She threw her head back. Maybe she'd been wrong. Maybe it was too much because she had never *felt* so much. He stretched her in a way she'd never experienced before. It was as if, finally, her body had met its match.

"You feel so good."

Good didn't quite describe it. Every withdrawal awoke nerves that Jolie had never known she had. Every thrust could be felt up inside her abdomen, sending wonderful tension into her chest and up into her throat as if the connection was deeper and more profound than any other.

And when Thad shifted, dragging one of her knees up and pressing it against her chest as he increased his tempo, Jolie was overcome with the sheer wholeness of Thad inside her. So full she couldn't imagine not having him there and how empty she would feel when he was gone.

"Thad." She panted his name. Pleading. For what? She didn't know exactly.

"Baby." The word was rough and ragged and Thad pressed down on her shoulder, giving him better leverage to thrust deeper and harder, just the way she loved it.

Could she come again so soon? Jolie had never done it before, but when Thad drove up into her she felt the orgasm building like she hadn't the first time, as if it started from her toes and ran up along her legs, gaining momentum until it pooled in her abdomen, growing and mounting. Three more quick thrusts followed by one hard one and Thad grunted loud and low, holding her hips flush. She'd never felt a man ejaculate before, but with Thad she did. His body pulsed right from the base of his cock. The pulses mimicked her own orgasm, so that Jolie couldn't tell whether the wonderful throbbing sensations were his or hers.

"Damn, girl," Thad murmured as he collapsed on top of her. "That was something else."

It *was* something else, and Jolie held on to him with arms and legs, because she wasn't ready to let him go.

However, a pounding on the outside door forced her to slacken her grip. Thad cursed softly under his breath and rolled off her. He grabbed a robe from the back of his bedroom door, shrugged into it and left the room.

"You going to help with chores today or what?" A deep voice floated in from the open doorway.

"Yeah. I'll be right there."

When Jolie heard the door close, she scooted out of bed, looking for her scattered clothes, feeling shy all of a sudden as she pulled on her panties and turned her back to the door to fasten her bra.

She felt his presence behind her. Felt his warmth as he leaned down close to her ear.

"You okay?"

"Mmm-hmm."

With gentle hands on her shoulders, he turned her to face him. "You sure?"

"Yes."

"You don't regret it?"

"No." And she didn't. Not one bit.

He smiled. "Good. Because if it wasn't for chores, we'd be doing *that* again."

SHOWERING AFTER CHORES gave Thad time to think about Jolie—more specifically, her gorgeous body pressed against his, her mouth drinking from his, her long, delicate fingers caressing his face. It wasn't good to be thinking about Jolie so much. He soaped his chest and under his arms, glancing down at the result of his thoughts.

"Sha…" Jolie Duval was trouble and he'd be best to stay away. He should have heeded Gloria's warnings.

But the woman was temptation incarnate and he'd never been good at abstaining.

Thad finished showering and dressed quickly, his hair still damp as he met Curtis outside the bunkhouse. The two of them walked over to the big house together, Curtis his usual silent self. Though the man wasn't much for chatter, Thad could tell he was pissed. Couldn't blame him. It wasn't like Thad to bugger off and spend the whole day playing hooky. Not that he regretted it. Hard to regret something that felt so damn good.

He shivered, running a hand through his damp hair, which was stiffening up in the frigid evening air. It reminded him of Jolie and how she'd nearly frozen to death earlier. Then again, everything reminded him of Jolie. It'd been a long time since he'd been this attracted to a woman.

And the last time had ended badly.

Which was why he was here, so far from home. Why he could never go back.

This was not good.

The door opened as they stood outside the house, stomping the snow from their boots.

"You're late," Gloria greeted them, hands on her hips. She had an extraspecial scowl for him.

Damn women and their freaky ability to know exactly what was going on at all times.

He followed her in, hung his jacket in the foyer closet and then all three made their way to the great room, where Gloria turned at the last second. "You even missed the surprise."

Jolie stood to the side of the room, a glass of wine in hand, her cheeks flushed, her eyes bright, wearing the sexiest red dress he'd ever seen. Not that it was low-cut or anything; it was made of some sort of knit material and clung to every blessed curve she had.

He tipped his head in her direction. It'd only been a few hours since he'd seen her—naked—and his body's reaction to her was instant.

If they were alone, he'd be ready to take her—hard—all over again.

He adjusted his stance, hoping to alleviate some of the pressure behind his fly, when someone clapped him on the back.

"Heya, Thad, how you been?"

Thad turned to find Dillon's younger brother, Colton, standing there, grinning, his arm around an older woman who Thad had never met before. "This is my mom, Catherine Cross. You should have seen Dillon's face when we showed up with Sage and Andy tonight."

So that was the surprise Gloria had been talking about. Dillon's family was here from Arizona.

"Nice to meet you," Thad said, giving Mrs. Cross a kiss on either cheek. Standing on the other side of them was Sage, an older woman who hailed from these parts, whom Thad greeted with a kiss, as well. Beside her stood her boyfriend, Andy, who happened to be Gloria's dad. Thad shook his hand and wished him a merry Christmas.

Because Thad and Curtis were late, the first course had already been laid out. The group of them, thirteen all told, sat down at the big table together.

Like one big family.

If only they knew who they had in their midst.

Jolie took the seat next to him, smiling shyly. Why did that sweet smile heat him up almost more than a seductive one would have? What did that say about him?

Gloria tapped her water glass and stood up. "Welcome, everyone. I just want to say a few words before we start."

Gloria was a tiny woman but she had a big presence, never more so than at that moment. "It's always been my dream to host big functions like this for family and friends." She lifted her glass to the guests. "This is such a special time of year and I am delighted that you chose to spend it with us, here at the ranch." Her chin quivered as she paused to swallow some emotion that came up faster than a summer storm.

Her gaze went to her husband and he reached for her free hand, giving her a squeeze and a nod of encouragement. She turned back to the group, her eyes liquid in the candlelight. "In honor of my late mother, who was of Italian descent, I've prepared a traditional Christmas Eve Feast of the Seven Fishes. Not easy to come by fresh seafood in the middle of Montana, let me tell you."

The group chuckled.

"If you're not a seafood fan, there will be plenty of other things to eat, too." She indicated the table, piled high with delicious-smelling dishes. "But I just wanted to say how happy I am—how very, very happy Dillon and I both are—that you're all here."

When her voice broke, she raised her glass in a toast. "And I'm sorry I'm all emotional, I just never imagined I could be this happy."

Dillon called, "Cheers," wrapping his arm around his tiny wife and rubbing her back with a tenderness that Thad had seen between the two right from the start.

Though things had been anything but smooth sailing between these two, that was for sure. In fact, it was a miracle they finally figured things out.

Thad found himself glancing at Jolie.

Why?

Certainly not because he wanted the same thing that

Dillon and Gloria had. Jolie was a holiday fling. That was it. End of story.

"Sage," Dillon said, "would you mind saying the blessing…"

Sage was a member of the Crow Nation, and when she was midway through the grace, which she gave in her own language, Thad heard a sniffle from right beside him. He opened his eyes to see Jolie, head bowed, with tears dripping off her chin. Without thinking twice about it, he reached for her hand and threaded his fingers through hers, holding tightly. He had no idea why she was crying, but he could guess. Hell, it was Christmas and here she was surrounded by strangers. It didn't take a genius to figure it out. Besides, wasn't he feeling melancholy himself? Maybe that's what this overpowering urge to be with Jolie was all about.

After the prayer ended, she slowly extricated her hand from his and wiped her damp cheek with her napkin. She turned to him and smiled.

"That was beautiful," she whispered, and the sadness he'd expected to see in her big eyes wasn't there. Instead, Jolie beamed, like she was one of the celestial beings from the Good Book, who heralded the birth of Christ himself.

How the hell was he going to stay away from her when all he could think about was tempting her into his arms like he was hoping to turn her into a fallen angel?

Thad turned back to the table and was greeted by a pointed stare from Gloria. So he did the only thing he could do: he lifted his glass and toasted her.

8

Travel tip: when you are out of your element, fake it.
>   Jo Duval

"YOU'RE LOST IN THOUGHT," Thad said as he took the seat beside her on the sofa while everyone made their way from the dining room into the great room.

"A little."

"You thinking of your family?"

She smiled wistfully. "That obvious?"

"Yep."

She patted her stomach, wanting to change the topic. "I'm also digesting. I am *so* full."

Thad's eyes lingered on her, his smile creeping up at the corners as his gaze drifted up to her face. Instantly, she felt the phantom sensations of their earlier tryst: his body flush with hers, his lips, his touch, his tongue…his body moving inside, making her feel completely full.

It was like he could read her mind because he leaned close and whispered, "Did I thank you properly for earlier?"

"No. You did not."

"Mmm." He sat back on the couch, a playful gleam in his eyes. "I thought I did."

"Nope."

"I feel like I need to thank you properly, then."

"Is that right?" Why was it so easy to banter with Thad?

"Don't you?"

"It would be the gentlemanly thing." She twisted her lips. "Though based on previous experience, I'm not sure that word accurately describes you."

He sat up straight, hand to chest. "I'm hurt."

"Thad," Gloria said, her voice curt as she approached, carrying a pitcher of punch in one hand and a plate of cookies in the other. "Would you mind refilling glasses?" Her smile looked fake.

"Duty calls." Thad winked and took the pitcher from Gloria. To the room, he said, "Did I ever tell y'all about how my dog Sue outsmarted the biggest, orneriest mountain lion these parts have ever seen?"

"No," Zak said with enthusiasm. "Tell us."

Jolie sipped her mulled wine as she listened to the story of the dog, Sue, luring a wild cat into a trap by faking an injury. Based on the way Gloria rolled her eyes, it was clearly a tall tale, though the story did make her smile and gaze lovingly at her husband. Jo scrutinized the interaction between Thad and Gloria, trying to figure out where the tension was coming from. Jolie thought back to when she arrived. The two had seemed friendly enough on that first night, but she'd been so scared by the dogs she might not have noticed tension. She certainly had ever since.

Why?

Puzzled, Jolie watched as Gloria made the rounds with the plate of cookies, so friendly with everyone except Thad. It was like she didn't trust him or something.

Once done offering cookies, Gloria set the plate down and went to stand beside the Christmas tree. "I was thinking it would be nice if we all shared some of our own Christmas traditions tonight. Last night we celebrated one of Thad's traditions." She smiled as she said his name, like she hadn't just been scowling at him. "Tonight we shared my traditional meal, and now—" she opened her arms wide, as if giving the whole room a hug "—I'd like to celebrate some of yours."

Oh, shit.

Jolie panicked, avoiding eye contact with Gloria, like she was back in middle school not wanting to be called on by a teacher when she hadn't done her homework.

Ridiculous.

"Jo? Was there something you wanted to share?"

Seriously?

She raised her head and forced a smile. "Too many traditions to come up with just one. Can you give me a second?"

"Of course."

"I've got one," Kaylee said. She got up from the love seat she shared with her husband, Evan, and proceeded to explain to Gloria what she wanted, pointing at the piano and the tree.

After Kaylee finished, Gloria nodded and turned to Dillon to talk quietly to him. Then she asked, "Catherine, you play, right?" She indicated the piano.

"I do," Catherine, Dillon's mother, rose from her chair, and Gloria explained what Kaylee wanted.

Moments later, Dillon returned with a well-worn copy of what could only be a bible, which Kaylee paged through while Gloria went and shut off the lights on the Christmas tree. When Kaylee found the passage she was looking for, she moved to the side of the piano and said, "Every Christmas Eve when I was a little girl, my dad would read the story of Christ's birth and my mom would play the piano and we…" Her voice trailed off as emotion took over. Evan jumped up and went to stand beside his new wife, wrapping his arm around her shoulders.

She beamed up at him, her lips wobbling in the process.

For no reason other than the fact that the moment was poignant, Jolie's throat constricted as Kaylee began to read in a wavering voice.

"'In those days Caesar Augustus issued a decree that a census should be taken of the entire Roman world...'"

Jolie listened, while moisture pricked the corners of her eyes. She knew the story—who didn't?—but it was the first time she'd heard it read like this, so softly and with such emotion. When Kaylee came to the part about Mary and Joseph journeying to Bethlehem, she paused, nodding to Catherine to play.

"O Little Town of Bethlehem, how still we see thee lie..." Everyone sang. Everyone knew the words.

Except her.

After the song ended, Kaylee kept reading. "'Mary wrapped her newborn son in cloths and placed him in a manger because there was no room for them in the inn...'" She paused again and Catherine started anew.

"Away in a manger, no crib for a bed..." the group sang.

Jolie sat completely still, observing as if she was on the outside looking in. She could pick out Dillon's voice—he had an amazing baritone—and marveled at how everyone sang with such certainty. The only other person who wasn't singing was Curtis.

When that song ended, Kaylee read some more, pausing every few minutes so that another carol could be sung.

"Angels We Have Heard on High."

"Hark the Herald Angels Sing."

Then "Joy to the World," at which time the lights of the Christmas tree were switched on. They seemed more brilliant and beautiful than before.

After Kaylee was done, everyone clapped and Gloria asked, "More carols?"

The group was in agreement and Catherine started in on a rousing rendition of "Jingle Bells," to which Zak sang his own words—"jingle bells, Batman smells, Robin laid an egg"—making Jolie smile. Of course she knew the words to "Jingle Bells," but she was enjoying just listening.

"Not much for singing?" Thad asked when he took his seat next to her again.

She shrugged.

"Singing's good for the soul, you know. Connects us to each other and…to the angels."

She raised a single brow at that comment. "Angels?"

"Don't tell me you don't believe in angels?"

"Not particularly."

He frowned. "Spirits?"

She shook her head.

"What about miracles?"

She shrugged. "They are simply people's way of explaining things they don't understand." Good Lord, it was like her mother had possessed her body and was speaking through her.

"You telling me you've never witnessed a real-life miracle?"

"Nope."

He shook his head sadly. "Now, that's too bad." He patted her hand. "But that shouldn't stop you from singing. It doesn't matter how good your voice is. All that matters is that you sing, for no other reason than that it feels good."

"Oh, I like to sing," Jolie said. She was no Dillon, but she wasn't half-bad.

"Then why aren't you?"

"It's a long story," she replied hesitantly.

"Long stories are the best kind."

"You won't believe me."

"Long and implausible stories are right up my alley."

Thad nudged her lightly. The innocent contact sent a wave of heat through her body.

"So…?" Thad moved so close his thigh was snugged right up against hers. He rested his hand on her leg and drew circular patterns, making her entire leg, right down to her toes, tingle.

She leaned close, like she had a secret, and whispered, "I don't know the words."

"What do you mean?" The drawing on her thigh stopped.

"I didn't grow up singing carols."

"Why's that?" Now he lightly drew on the back of her hand. "Are you Jewish? Duval doesn't sound Jewish." He started caressing again.

"No…" She paused, enjoying his touch so much she almost couldn't remember what she was talking about. "My family didn't go to church, so…"

Thad waited for her to continue. When she didn't he said, "So?"

She shrugged. "I don't know the religious carols."

He blinked and waited some more. His blue eyes narrowed. "That's it?" His hand stopped moving again.

"Pretty much."

"By definition, a long story consists of more than six words."

She gazed at where his hand rested on top of hers, wishing he would start caressing again, because it felt so nice.

"And…as a non-churchgoer, you don't listen to the radio?"

She made a face. "Of course I do."

"So you have to know *some* Christmas songs. Maybe you haven't noticed," he leaned close and whispered, "but they're the same ones every year."

She rolled her eyes. "I do know some." Jolie worked

her hand out from under his so she could touch him. So strong. So…

Focused on his hand, she traced over the top of the largest vein—why were the veins in his hands sexy?—while absently rattling off the titles of her favorite classics. A flash of his strong hands holding her wrists above his head made her gasp. Oh, yes. That would be why.

But then she remembered how tender he could be, too, how he'd taken care of her when she was freezing cold.

"I know 'Baby, It's Cold Outside.' Is that a Christmas song?" she asked softly.

"Sure, why not. You know all the words to it?"

"Mmm-hmm." She touched the space between his thumb and forefinger. Even this part of him was muscular.

"That's good enough for me." Thad climbed to his feet and pulled her up with him. There was a break in the music, and turning to the room, he said, "Ms. Jolie and I would like to take a turn at singing a duet."

"Um, Thad? What are you doing?"

He winked at her and pulled her closer to the piano.

"I'm not going to sing in front of everyone," she hissed.

He ignored her protest. "Ms. Catherine, do you know 'Baby, It's Cold Outside'?"

She frowned and shook her head.

"That's fine, we'll sing a cappella."

"Wait." Jolie tugged on his hand. "A cappella?"

"Yep. Unless you know how to play."

Actually, she did. She'd only been playing piano since she was seven years old. Taking a seat at the bench, she rested her fingers on the keys, attempting to conjure up the music. She played a chord, then another, deciding on the key.

"You've been holding out on us," Thad chided softly.

Her response was a pretend scowl. "Do you know all the words?"

"Of course," he said with a twinkle glimmering in his blue eyes as he leaned against the piano. "For the most part."

"I can't believe you're making me do this." Yet here she was, deciding on the key of C major, ready to sing, as if she really was this person she was pretending to be.

She finished playing the introduction to the song, paused, nodded at Thad and then sang softly, "I really can't stay…"

"Baby, it's cold outside…" His voice sent shivers down her spine.

"I've got to go 'way…"

"Baby, it's cold outside…" As they continued to sing, those shivers raced right back up to the crown of her head.

How was it possible that their voices complemented one another as well as their bodies had earlier in the day? Hers soft and his strong? Both a little rough around the edges, but it didn't matter. They sang the chorus in harmony as if they'd performed together for years. Jolie completely forgot that they were surrounded by a room of people, and sang to Thad as if they were having a private, flirty conversation through song. There was a point where Thad didn't know the words and just ad-libbed his way through it: "Don't know the words to this part…keep singing or you'll break my heart…"

Laughing, Jolie kept on until Thad picked up the lyrics again. For the last verse, he sat beside her on the bench, threw an arm across her shoulders and held her close for the final "Oh, baby, it's cold outside!"

She couldn't help herself; she leaned against him and dissolved into laughter while the room exploded with applause. They returned to the couch and fell back into the soft leather, Jolie feeling warm and tingly and wonderful.

"That was fun," Thad rumbled quietly.

"It was."

"You've a pretty voice on you." He picked up her hand. "And talent in these soft hands."

"You're not so bad yourself." She elbowed him gently in the ribs, and his arm came around her shoulder. Possessive and sweet all at once. How was it possible to feel so comfortable, so safe and warm and wonderful, with a man she'd just met? Particularly since they were surrounded by a room full of virtual strangers?

Maybe she did believe in miracles.

"Dad?" Zak asked in the lull between songs. "What about *our* Christmas story?"

"Sorry, bud. I don't have the book," Simon said, giving Zak an apologetic rub on the top of his head.

"I bet you know it. You've been reading it to me every night for the last week."

A few others in the room piped up with encouragement for Simon to recite the story.

"Really," Simon insisted, obviously becoming uncomfortable. "I don't know it off by heart."

"I'll help," Zak said. He stood in front of the whole group, tugged down on his sleeves and in an overly loud voice, began reciting the beginning of *How the Grinch Stole Christmas*.

Between the whole group of them, they managed to get through the entire story, and even Jolie remembered a few lines. Halfway through, Zak climbed onto his father's lap, his cheeks rosy, his eyes drooping as he tucked his head beneath his father's chin. Such a different kid than the one who'd run around earlier, like Thad's dogs, with boundless energy.

Catherine smiled warmly, giving Dillon a not-so-subtle raised eyebrow as she looked from father and son back to Dillon and then over to Gloria. "Why don't we sing 'Silent Night'?" she suggested.

Thad's arm remained around Jolie's shoulders as Catherine played a chord and then let the group sing the song a cappella. It was beautiful and for the third time that night, she felt tears pooling in her eyes.

This was it. *This* was the Christmas she'd always wanted, always longed for. Yes, her family spent "the holiday" together, but their traditions didn't include parties and stories and sharing. They included taking shifts that no one else wanted at the hospital because everyone else was celebrating. Yes, they shared a nice meal and always donated to a charity of choice, but they spent the meal discussing work and big issues: war, politics, the injustices in the world. They'd debate practical ways they could all do something to make a difference. It was all well-intentioned and there was nothing wrong with it…exactly. Jolie rubbed her cheek, trying to figure out why she'd always felt like she was missing something in the way her family celebrated the holidays.

Maybe that was it. It *wasn't* a celebration.

And Jolie had always longed for festivities like tonight's.

She wanted lights, decorations, trees and garlands. She wanted traditions that were passed on based on religion or family or that somehow harkened back to their countries of origin, like the Feast of the Seven Fishes or Tip's Eve. Speaking of which, she liked to get *tipsy*, laugh, hang mistletoe, play games, tell stories…

"C'mon, Zak," Gloria said. "We'd better set out cookies."

"Wait." Zak clung to his father. "Where's my stocking? Did we bring my stocking?"

Gloria pointed to the mantel, where a row of stockings were hung. They were so pretty. "There's thirteen of them. One for each of us."

Eyeing the stockings all tacked up in a row, Jolie was suddenly struck by a memory of being very young and spending Christmas with her father's parents in Wisconsin. Her mother had stayed to work in the ER, and her father had taken Jolie and her brother back to visit relatives. He hadn't been particularly close to his parents and they'd died shortly after—a heart attack and a stroke, for which he blamed their excessive drinking—but she remembered that Christmas now.

Family and friends had crowded into their old house. The smell of the wood-burning fire, the tree and all the presents underneath. She even remembered the stockings hung up along that fireplace. Oh, she'd been so excited!

How could she have forgotten that?

Maybe because she'd been so young.

She pinched the bridge of her nose, trying to remember what happened next. A vague recollection of her father arguing with her grandfather surfaced and then…oh, yes. Sitting in the car and driving back home in the middle of the night. Jo remembered crying because all she'd wanted was to wake up on Christmas morning to a stocking filled with gifts like all the other kids.

That was the last time she'd seen her grandparents before they died. It was also the night she realized there was no Santa. No magic. No Christmas.

Tonight, however, Jolie wanted to believe again. The very thought of it made her smile.

"Can I tell you something?" Thad said huskily as he squeezed her hand.

"Sure."

"You are a beautiful woman, but when you smile you take my breath away."

She head butted his shoulder and Thad took the opportunity to lean in close to her ear and whisper, "Do me a favor, will you?"

The warm air inside her ear sent delicious shivers down her spine, and the vibrations of his deep voice got her heart pounding. "Depends on what it is," she answered softly.

"Leave those French doors of yours open tonight."

She pulled back to look at him. "What are you suggesting, Mr. Knight?"

"If Santa Claus is allowed to break into people's houses, why not me?"

She bit gently on her lower lip. "Because Santa is a gentleman. And you?" She poked his chest. "Are not."

9

Travel tip: sometimes the sexiest lingerie is no lingerie.

Jo Duval

IT WAS CHRISTMAS EVE—well, technically it was Christmas morning because it was 1:00 a.m.—and Jolie was snuggled beneath the comforter of her queen-size bed, giddy. Was this what it was like to be a kid, lying in bed, wide-awake in hope of catching the sound of Santa's sled on the roof? Listening for the telltale sound of footsteps or hooves? Hoping to hear the tinkle of sleigh bells?

She giggled.

Not because she was tipsy—okay, she was a little tipsy—but because she had a surprise for dear old Santa. Her hands went to her stomach, one going up the other going down, touching herself—her naked self. Yep, she was waiting for *Santa* with bells on and that was it.

She'd gone through her luggage even though she knew exactly what was there, or rather what *wasn't* there. Sexy sleepwear was nowhere to be found. So, as far as she was concerned, this was the next best thing.

Rolling over, she touched the screen of her cell to check the time.

One fifteen.

Still nothing.

She flopped onto her back, replaying the whole day in her head. The sleigh ride to the ghost town—fun. The trip back—not as much fun. Warming up at Thad's place—nice. His naked body and her naked body—very nice...

She rubbed her knees together.

Her thoughts lingered there for a few minutes before drifting to other things: the delicious meal, the evening spent with a group of strangers. Her topsy-turvy emotions.

Pushing herself up to her elbows, she strained to hear something—anything—but there was nothing.

Maybe Thad wasn't coming. Maybe he'd had second thoughts.

She rolled to her other side, playing with a string on the handmade quilt. What if he didn't come? How would she feel? As disappointed as she'd been leaving her grandparents' place in the middle of the night?

Her bare arm suddenly felt cold on the outside of the blanket and she tucked it back inside.

What are you doing, Jolie?

Fine time for her inner critic to be up and chiding her, reminding her she was lying in bed, *naked*, waiting for a man she'd just met.

Jolie sat up, pressing her hands to her face. She was setting herself up for heartache. She was a fool to think she could do this without getting emotionally invested, particularly at Christmas time.

Dum, dum, dum, dum, dum.

Wait, what was that?

Jolie tilted her head, straining to hear.

Was that the crunch of boots on snow?

Her pulse quickened, which made picking up sounds from outside difficult because all she could hear was the pounding of her pulse inside her ears. She waited, consciously slowing her breath, moving her hair back so that her ear was free.

When there was no more sound, no crunching of snow or tapping on the glass, no sliding of the door, she realized it must have been her imagination.

"You are a fool, Jolie Duval," she whispered to herself. "A sentimental, romantic fool."

THADDEUS TILTED HIS FACE to the sky as big, fluffy flakes settled on his cheeks. What the hell was he doing here? It was Christmas Eve, for fuck's sake. He should not be out gallivanting tonight of all nights, particularly not with a woman like Jolie Duval. Gloria had been right to warn him off. As much as the writer from Chicago liked to pretend she was worldly, after tonight he could tell she was anything but. How many times had he caught her sniffing away emotion? Blotting unshed tears? She was not the type to have an affair that meant nothing, which was the number one thing he looked for in the women he took to bed.

The strange thing was, he didn't want her any different. When her big doe eyes got all bright with nostalgia, or whatever the hell it was, he'd been overcome with an urge to wrap her up in his arms and hold her tight. Yet, minutes later, when she'd crooned to him in that soft and sexy voice, he'd had the same urge, to hold her tightly in his arms...

And then take off her clothes and do unspeakable things between those incredible long legs.

Scrubbing a hand across his cheek, Thad gazed at the French doors leading to her bedroom. There she was, just inside, the sweetest, sexiest Christmas present he could ask for. As far as he figured, he had a choice, and he needed to make it, right here, right now. He could either open those doors, wrap his arms around Jolie like he'd wanted to all night and make love to her, helping her forget her soul-deep loneliness, because he understood it though he'd be damned if he admitted it. But if he followed through with such a plan, he'd likely be making the *second* biggest mistake of his life.

And a man like him could not afford another big mistake.

No. Best he turn around, go back to bed and wake up tomorrow much like he had every Christmas since fleeing NOLA. Alone. No attachments, no entanglements.

No questions.

A light came on behind the closed blinds.

Shit.

Her face appeared, peering out between the slats of the blinds. Could she see him?

The door slid open a crack.

"You out there?"

He should have hightailed it while he had the chance, because now it was too late.

Except a part of him was glad. A big part.

"Heya, Jolie."

"What are you doing?" She had a robe wrapped tight around her as she poked her head outside.

"Just enjoying the quiet."

"Oh."

He wiped the snow off the lid of the hot tub, knowing he should be contemplating alternatives but only able to think about one thing: Jolie, and what he might find beneath her robe.

"Did you want to have a hot tub?"

"Naw." He took two steps toward her.

"Is everything okay?"

He hated how tentative she sounded, like she'd doubted he would show up. Even though he almost hadn't. He didn't like being a disappointment. And he particularly didn't like disappointing this woman, no matter what his logic center was saying.

"Everything's just fine." Another measured step, then another until he was face-to-face with her.

"Did you still want to come in?"

"Are you inviting me in?"

She hesitated, then smiled. "Yes, I am."

"Then let's go."

She backed away from the door so that he could enter, and the first thing he did after sliding the door closed behind him was take off his boots.

The second he stood up, she grabbed the front of his parka and pulled him close, planting a deliciously warm kiss on his cold lips. "I've wanted to do that all night."

"You and me both."

She smiled up at him, a wide, radiant expression that once more drew his attention to her lovely mouth.

Seriously, that *mouth*.

"You have the nicest mouth, did you know that?" He ran a thumb across. "I can't stop thinking about it."

"Is that so?"

"Yes." Was she purposefully tempting him by rubbing her lips together?

"Hmm." She backed up to the bed, watching him, playing with the ties on her robe. Her eyes glistened in the lamplight, not with melancholy but with playfulness.

"Go ahead," he rasped.

"Go ahead and what?"

"Take it off."

Instead of untying the ties, she tightened them. "You first."

Thad groaned. The sweet Jolie from earlier in the evening was nowhere to be found and a vixen had taken her place.

"You drive a hard bargain, miss."

"Shut up and strip." She pointed. "Now."

"Bossy."

"Uh-huh."

He unzipped his parka and tossed it onto a nearby chair. Then he took a couple steps toward her. "You gonna help?"

"Nope. Just gonna watch." She sat on the edge of the bed.

"You're wicked, you know that?"

Her smile told him he had yet to see the exact degree her wickedness could reach, and Thad had to quell the urge to tear his clothes off, stalk up to her, rip open her robe like he was tearing tissue paper from a gift and take her the way she said she liked it. *Hard and fast.* He paused to suck in a deep breath. The mere thought of it sent blood pounding between his legs.

He started in on the buttons on his shirt: one, two, three. Pause.

Four, five, six.

"Keep going."

Yanking on the bottom of his shirt, he pulled it from his jeans and finished the last few buttons before shrugging out of it, not even bothering to toss it, but dropping it on the floor. With both hands on the bottom of his undershirt, he pulled it over his head.

There was something satisfying about hearing her gasp at the sight of his chest. Thad moved closer, just in case she was of a mind to touch. He glanced at her hands, where her fingers played with the ties of the robe. He could almost feel them on his skin. Delicate and soft. Tentative and teasing.

Good God, he needed to unzip his fly because he almost couldn't breathe from the pressure building behind it.

One more step and he was knee to knee with her. Needing to get closer, he straddled her legs so that his crotch hovered right above where her hands rested in her lap. Tugging on his belt buckle, he asked, "You sure you don't want to do this for me?"

While her head moved back and forth in denial, her fingers seemed to have other ideas. She dropped the ties of her robe in order to caress the outside of his thighs.

Nice.

"I got a job for you," he said through clenched teeth because her touch felt so damn good.

"That right?"

"Yep." He twisted his right hip toward her. "Reach in that pocket there."

She did as he asked, her hand slithering deep inside to where he'd stuck a row of condoms.

"Put those on that bedside table for me, would you?"

Ever so slowly, she withdrew her hand, pulling out the four-pack of condoms with it. With an arched brow, she held them up with the tips of her fingers. "Four? Rather presumptuous, don't you think?"

"I prefer to think of it in terms of being prepared for *all* eventualities."

Laughing, she deposited the condoms on the bedside table while he popped his belt buckle. Then he captured her left hand and placed it over the bulge at the front of his jeans. She may have said she didn't want to help, but as far as Thad was concerned, there was nothing sexier than soft fingers working a zipper. Nothing more arousing than a feminine hand searching down inside behind his fly, coming in contact with his inflamed flesh.

"Oh, my," she breathed, her small hand doing exactly what he'd imagined, wrapping tight around his erection.

She squeezed—blessed girl—and then tugged her hand out of his shorts to grip the waistband of his jeans. The denim didn't want to cooperate, and Thad had to move out of range in order to strip them off because he needed the blasted jeans gone. *Right now.*

Clad in only his boxers, he moved in again, taking her elbows and urging her to her feet, his hands resting on the ties to her robe before undoing the knot. "I wonder what we have under here?"

She pretended to slap his hands away but not before he got the ties undone and the robe spread.

"Lord have mercy," Thad gritted out, taking in her gorgeous body.

The robe slid off her shoulders and she stood there, bathed in lamplight, his very own contradiction. An angel, a vixen, a sweet-tempered seductress.

As if to prove his point, she turned and gave him a gentle shove, pushing him onto the bed before climbing up after. To think he'd only seen her as all flailing arms and legs when he'd first met her. That image seemed laughable now because this woman moved with lithe grace, her honey-brown hair swishing across her shoulders as she straddled him.

She lowered herself, bare chest to bare chest, her soft breasts like sweet pillows between them. "You like my mouth, huh?" Was she purposefully biting down on her full lower lip? Probably.

Beautiful, wanton woman.

Thad couldn't help himself. Taking a fistful of hair, he yanked her close and kissed her open mouth. So warm. So wet. So provocative. She wriggled deliciously on top of him and his other hand went low to her bare ass, pulling that part of her close, too. Only his boxer shorts keeping them from each other.

Twisting her head out of his grasp, Jolie met his gaze. "What is it *exactly* about my mouth that you like?"

Cupping her chin, he tugged on her lower lip and she sucked his thumb into her mouth, swirling her tongue around it, never breaking eye contact with him. Was she hoping to see some kind of reaction? Couldn't she feel it rising between them?

She covered his hands with hers and pulled his thumb slowly from the warm cavern of her mouth. Then she licked the tip of one finger and the next. With her lips parted, she moved her mouth back and forth across his fingertips, licking and dipping, miming the very thing he was hoping she'd do with another—very aroused—part of him.

"Do you like that?"

"Yes."

Her smile was pure sex before she dipped low, taking his fingers deep into her mouth before withdrawing, nice and slow, sucking hard while Thad cursed a blue streak under his breath. A fleeting smile flashed before she moved on, nibbling his jaw on a path for his ear. "What else do you like?" she whispered hotly.

"Whatever you want."

"Really?" She slithered lower, nipping at his neck and biting his collarbones. Lord help him, the woman was a wild carnivore cloaked in the skin of some gentle fawn. A sweet and sexy paradox.

What she did next was an almost exact repeat of the fantasy he'd had in the shower. Her mouth on his chest, sucking his nipple. Hard. Licking the lines between his abs, back and forth, the touch made more sensual by the swish of hair that followed her tongue.

She stopped when she came to his pelvis.

Lying on one side of his legs, Jolie followed the line of hair from his navel down to the waistband of his shorts. Dipping beneath, she ran her fingers horizontally along his belly, grazing the tip of his cock.

With one finger, she drew a line down the center of his erection, the touch more excruciating because it was over the top of his boxers. For the moment, Thad was content to watch her gentle, almost innocent exploration of him. However, when her fingers ventured beneath the waistband of his boxers again, it was more than he could take and he lifted his hips, needing her to take them off.

Which she did, thank God.

"You're as handsome here as everywhere else," she said, gazing down at his engorged cock.

Cheeky girl, repeating what he'd said to her earlier in the day.

But her cheekiness did not end there. Hell no. Those delicate fingers of her tickled the sensitive skin on either side of his erection, his cock jumping toward her hand, pleading with her to touch.

She ignored him.

"You trying to kill me, girl?"

"Maybe," she said, licking the tip of her finger before softly drawing a line down the full length of his penis.

Torture.

But when sweet Jolie wrapped her cool hand around his cock and kissed the tip of him, his mind went blank. All he could do was watch and feel. The same tongue that had swirled around his thumb swirled around the head of his cock. That lovely wide mouth opened over him, not touching—oh, no—but breathing hot, damp air over him. No contact but ever so close.

The need to thrust overcame him and he lifted his hips. Needing that mouth. Needing that tongue. Needing suction and heat and warmth and everything else.

Needing her.

"What do you want, Thad?" she whispered, gazing up at him from between his legs.

"You, baby."

"Which part of me?" Her eyes were hooded with desire and she licked her lips with exaggerated purpose. Seductive. Wanton. Beautiful.

"Whichever part you want."

And there it was, that luminous smile he couldn't get enough of, but it disappeared when she bent low in order to lick his length. Thad jerked involuntarily. The woman was in danger of turning him into something so far removed from a gentleman that it scared him. He was on the verge of becoming the man he hadn't been in a very long time.

"Tell me," she urged, circling his head again.

Thad groaned. She shouldn't be doing this. No matter how good it felt.

Jolie licked her hand and wrapped the damp palm around his shaft, moving it up and down. "Is this what you want?"

Yes. That felt good, but what was even better was when she lowered herself again so that her mouth remained open on top, so that with every upward movement of her hand, the tip of him entered that blessed space.

"Say it, Thad."

He groaned, long and low, and then found the words. "Your mouth. I need your mouth, Jolie."

10

While on vacation, don't be afraid to ask for what you want. As long as you ask nicely.

Jo Duval

JOLIE HAD NEVER felt more in control, more powerful, more feminine. Just as she lowered her mouth over him and sucked, Thad threaded his fingers through her hair, a desperate act, and ground his pelvis up, moaning guttural and low.

How was this possible? How did she, Jolie Duval, have this ability to make a man desperate? To make him groan in ecstasy? Had she always had it?

Who cared. She had it now, and she was about to take full advantage of it.

She pulled back, sucking as she went, and then dropped down again, going deeper. The result was a whole string of nonsensical curse words interspersed with grunts of pleasure.

She had never elicited such sounds from a man before. It was hot.

Jolie got lost in it all, enjoying not only Thad's response to her mouth but the pure pleasure of the act. How it made her feel alive, excited, powerfully aroused.

When Jo finally lifted her head, she was met with a man

who appeared almost feral: his nostrils flared, his cheeks flushed and his teeth bared.

"Enough," he growled.

In one swift movement Thad flipped her so that he was lying on top of her. He pinned her hands and between clenched teeth said, "You like to tease men to death, do you?"

Was that what he thought of her? That she did this all the time?

She shook her head, though she couldn't shake the smile, because the idea of her, Jolie Duval, as a shameless tease was pretty damn funny.

"So it's true." Thad nudged her thighs wide, still holding her arms down.

"Nope." Her smile must have said otherwise.

"Who are you?" His gaze softened and so did his grip as his mouth descended over hers. "Who the hell are you?"

Thad's lips were soft as they slanted over hers, yet his tongue was insistent as he pushed it into her mouth. He released her hands to cup her face and hold her so he could kiss her the way he wanted, with an open, giving mouth, becoming more wild and ravenous by the second.

"I am in desperate need of a condom but I don't want to move," he murmured against her lips.

Blindly, Jolie reached toward the bedside table, knocking her phone off in the process, but thankfully finding what she was looking for on the second pass. She passed the condoms to Thad, who groaned as he rolled off her, lying on his back beside her as he tore open a packet.

She played with herself while he rolled on a rubber and when he turned back toward her, he took hold of her hand—which she'd had wedged between her legs—and licked her fingers.

Jolie was sure she'd died and gone to heaven.

When he was done, he moved back on top of her. "Now, where were we?" He kissed her. "Mmm. This feels about right."

Jolie adjusted her hips beneath him before taking hold of him and guiding him to her entrance. With a grunt, Thad looked up. He smoothed hair from her forehead and gazed into her eyes as he thrust, entering her slowly, inch by magnificent inch.

"I was mistaken." His voice was rough. "Now, *this* feels about right."

She couldn't agree more. But neither did she question why Thad's body, fully seated inside of hers, felt so right. He stayed there for a few breaths, simply staring into her eyes, a serious expression on his face, then his lids slid shut and his mouth descended on hers. The stillness of the moment passed as Thad kissed her, withdrawing and then thrusting with more force, while his tongue did the same.

Once, twice, three times.

He lifted his head in order to take a few deep breaths.

"Again," Jolie panted, clutching his ass with both hands, pulling while she lifted her hips.

"Woman, you keep that up and I'm not going to last."

"It's okay," she said, tugging again.

"No. It's not." Thad rolled off her so that he could lie by her side. "You have any idea how close you got me." He dragged a finger from her lower lip, down her chin and throat to her breasts.

"No," she murmured, loving the rough texture of his fingers on her skin.

He played with a nipple, twisting gently before lowering for a kiss. His hand kept on its downward journey to her stomach and then to her hip. "You make me feel like a randy teenager."

"Is that good?"

"Oh, baby. You have no idea." His fingers inched lower, massaging her clit, while he continued to suck on her nipple.

"I might have—" she gasped "—some idea." And she did, because he was driving her mental with his tongue and touch.

"I doubt it." He parted her pussy lips, stroking her there, spreading arousal with the flat of his hand.

"Thad…"

"You drive me crazy." He corkscrewed two fingers inside of her, making her moan. He pressed his thumb down on her clit, in that way she loved, while he worked another finger inside of her.

"Thad, I'm not kidding…"

"Neither am I." He bit her nipple while moving his hand faster between her legs.

It was wonderful. Excruciatingly wonderful.

"Please."

"Please what, sweetheart?" He wriggled his fingers inside of her until she was writhing beneath him.

"Oh, please!" Her hips flew off the bed, meeting his hand, thrust for thrust as she rolled her head back and forth across the pillow in delicious frustration.

"You're not the only one who can tease."

"Thad!"

He withdrew his hand and climbed back on top of her. "Say it." His voice was low and formidable.

"Say what?"

"Tell me what you're begging for." He wedged his thigh between her legs and moved it back and forth creating wonderfully frustrating friction.

It was too good. Too much. She writhed beneath him and begged, "Make love to me. Please, Thad. Make love to me."

He stilled.

Jo did, too. She opened her eyes and gazed up into his face. Stone cold and serious.

Had she said the wrong thing?

Thad's expression changed; it softened into a gentle frown before an irreverent light came into his eyes. "Seeing as you asked so nicely…"

He moved quickly, so quickly she wasn't prepared. Flipping her onto her tummy, Thad raised her hips, pulled her close and thrust.

All the way.

There it was!

Elbows on the bed, her ass in the air, the new position sent brand-new vibrations through her, igniting a bonfire to show Thad the way home. And he found it. Again and again and again. One hand tightened on her shoulder and the other gripped her hip as he pulled her close for one last thrust, his body jerking behind hers just as she saw starbursts behind her own closed lids.

"Jo-lie…" His breath was ragged in her ear as he covered her back with his body, holding her close. Keeping her in his arms, he rolled the two of them together to their sides. They lay there panting as Thad absently caressed her hip.

After a few minutes, Thad snuggled her against him, sighing into her hair and murmuring words of wonder and contentment.

Holy.

In, out. In, out. Jolie was still in the process of catching her breath,

What the hell had just happened?

Um…the best sex of her life, that's what.

THAD STOOD NAKED at the bathroom sink, the water running, staring at his reflection.

"What the hell are you doing?" he asked the man in the mirror.

No answer.

Figured.

For a man who always had answers, even if that answer was *run!*, not knowing what to do was a very bad sign. For over a decade, Thad had lived by a very strict set of rules, ones that only he was privy to. They included never getting involved with a woman past one night of pleasure. So, what had happened?

Make love to me.

He could still hear her voice, like she was standing right behind him, whispering. One part sweetness, the other part harlot. The two sides of her a delicious combination that he couldn't get enough of.

He splashed cold water on his face and then used the towel beside the sink to dry off. It smelled like peppermint. Like her.

Running his hand through his already messy hair, Thad groaned. Well, he'd just have to go out there and make it clear to her about how things were going to go between them. If she wasn't okay with that, he'd best say goodbye tonight before things got any worse.

Or…any better.

Turning off the light, Thad exited the bathroom and made his way to the bed, where Jolie was sitting up, the covers pulled up under her chin, looking like sweet temptation all over again. His gaze flicked to the remaining condoms on the bedside table and his cock twitched in reflexive excitement.

Down, boy.

"Hey," Jolie said softly, gnawing shyly on her lip.

Oh, dear God. That woman had to stop drawing his attention to her sweet, sweet mouth. He eyed the clothes strewn all over the floor, with half a mind to get dressed and bolt. But instead he flipped the sheets back and crawled into bed beside her, having no desire to be anywhere else.

The second he was under the covers, she slid close, putting her head on his chest and draping a long, lovely leg over his.

Thad inhaled deeply, bolstering himself for the conversation they needed to have.

"Tell me about your family," he said.

What? Where the hell had that come from?

She was so quiet he didn't think she was going to answer, and he stroked the back of her head to comfort her.

"There's not much to tell, really."

"What happened to them?"

Her hand stopped playing with the hair on his chest as she raised her head to frown at him. "What do you mean?"

"How did they die?"

"Die?" She made a sound at the back of her throat. "They didn't die."

He blinked. "Then what the hell are you doing here?"

Tilting her head to one side, she said, "I'm on assignment."

"Over Christmas?"

"Yes."

"And you'd rather spend Christmas with strangers than with family?"

She frowned, blinked and then settled her head on his chest once more. "Yes." She sounded defensive.

"Don't get along?" he asked softly, rolling his eyes at himself. What on earth was possessing him to keep asking these personal questions? What he should be doing was clearing the air between them, not getting to know her better.

Her delicate fingers started up on his chest again, gliding over skin and twirling in amongst the hair.

"We get along fine. I'm just sort of…the black sheep of the family."

Thad laughed, a single sharp bark. "You? A black sheep? C'mon."

"Don't laugh." She pinched his nipple, which only made him laugh more. "It's true."

"What have *you* done to become the black sheep in your family?"

"It's not what I've done." Her chest rose and fell heavily against him. "More like what I *haven't* done."

"So, what *haven't* you done?"

"Made something of myself. Done something meaningful with my life…found purpose."

Fitting his knuckle beneath her chin, he raised her face to his. "What on God's green earth are you talking about? You *are* someone special."

Her smile was wistful. "No. I'm not."

"What? Is your family made up of a bunch of superheroes or something?"

"Pretty much." She nestled back on his chest, her head fitting perfectly in the hollow of his shoulder beneath his chin. "My mom's head of ER at Northwestern Memorial. She saves lives every day. My dad's a neurosurgeon at Rush Medical. He saves lives every day. My brother's a district attorney for Cook County. He's dedicated his life to protecting the good people from the rapists and murderers and hardened criminals in this world." She paused. "Then there's me. What do I do? I write travel articles. Fluff. Stuff that is unnecessary and lacks meaning."

"Is that what they say?"

She was quiet again. "No. But it's clear in what they don't say."

"Because you're not saving lives?" Good Lord, what would her family make of him? Thad dared not think about it. "Not everyone can be a doctor or a lawyer. Think how boring that would make the world."

She laughed softly and the movement of her body felt good against his.

"You are anything but boring." He stroked the soft skin of her back. "I'm sure they see that."

"It's not about being boring or not. It's about having purpose. You know how I told you I didn't go to church?"

"Yeah?"

"Well, it's more than that. My family's staunchly secular humanist."

"So?"

"So, when you believe you are here on earth purely as a biological statistic—tantamount to winning the lottery at a-trillion-to-one odds—and that this is the one and only life you'll ever lead, then you damn well better make the most of it. Because luck combined with life should not be wasted."

"Hmm. An interesting supposition."

"It's my family credo."

"So, you're not living up to your potential?" Thad chuckled sardonically. If only he could tell her what a disappointment he was. No—calling himself that was mild compared to what he truly was. Thad was the definition of a black sheep, the real deal.

"I'm supposed to be a reporter, breaking big stories… not some travel writer…" Her words trailed off. "I don't know why I'm telling you all this."

"It's okay. I like knowing where you come from." Thad realized his mistake too late.

"What about you?"

"Not much to tell, really." Shit. Of course she'd turn

it around and want to know. Well, if there was one thing Thad was good at, it was making up stories. The trick was to start with truth, then embellish and add enough stuff so that it was as plausible as real life, but not too implausible.

"Well, you're a long way from home, cowboy." She'd put on a Southern drawl as she propped her chin on her hands to gaze up at him.

"I suppose."

"When did you leave?" she asked.

"Like everyone else. Right after Katrina."

"What about your family?"

"My parents died in a boating incident when I was little. Was raised by my grandmere." He hadn't thought of her in such a long time because he never let himself. When she did happen to cross his mind, it was always in terms of someone else's grandmother, from a distance, because the last time he'd seen her, he disappointed her in ways that would haunt him forever.

He could imagine the shock on Jolie's face when he tried to explain. The disbelief, followed by horror. Then disgust.

"Is she still alive? Your grandmother?"

"Naw. Casualty of Katrina."

"Oh, Thad. I'm so sorry." She rubbed a circle over his heart.

"I shoulda stayed with her, or convinced her to leave." This was both the truth and a lie. He could have stayed. Then he'd have died with her and that would have been the end of it. But instead he ran, and he did it without any thought of taking her with him, not that she would have gone.

"No one knew how bad it was going to be," she said softly.

"People knew." Fuck. He knew. And he'd been thankful for the pending disaster. Not because of how bad it would be or that it would kill his grandmother but because he'd hoped it would get the Feds off his tail.

And it had. He was one of the presumed dead. Thank God. And he had to keep it that way.

"I'm sorry."

He heaved a sigh because he had just told Jolie Duval more than he'd told anyone about himself since he'd left. "Naw, I'm sorry."

"It must be hard at this time of year. With no family." Now she was rubbing the scar on his shoulder and all the memories that Thad had buried bubbled up to the surface.

His grandmere, telling him to stay away from the Salvatori family and especially Raina. Beautiful, spoiled Raina. How he hadn't listened and had proposed to her on Christmas Eve—God, that was twelve years ago now. How he'd thought the family had accepted him when she'd said yes.

Except they hadn't. Not until he proved himself.

Oh, God.

The things they'd wanted him to do. What he'd done…

"You okay?"

"Sorry. I just don't like talking about it much. You understand?"

"Sure." She was still again, the kind of stillness that meant her brain was working extrahard, which meant more questions were pending.

He should just get up and leave, right now. But that would only make someone like Jolie think about his situation even harder, and he couldn't have that. There was only one way Thad knew to get someone's brain to shut off, to make them forget.

He scooched down beneath the covers, rolled the two of them over so he was on top of her again and kissed her. She wasn't the only one who needed to forget. Thad needed to as well, because he had no time to be haunted by the ghosts of Christmas past.

It was too dangerous.

11

I've never really understood the saying Home Is Where the Heart Is…until today.

Jo Duval

JOLIE AWOKE TO the sound of squeals, which brought an automatic smile to her face. Then other memories surfaced—vigorous, satisfying memories—and her smile grew. She reached for Thad, even though she knew he was gone. Maybe she was hoping for some lingering warmth. She wrapped her arms around the pillow he'd used and sniffed.

Mmm. Smoke and cedar and soap and Thad.

While he'd tried to quietly dress when he left in the wee hours of the morning, she'd heard him anyway. Just as he'd opened the French doors, but before he could step outside, she'd called, "Merry Christmas."

With his back still to her, he waited and then slowly turned. She hadn't been able to make out his features in the darkness. "Merry Christmas to you, too, Jolie Duval."

"I'll see you later?"

"Of course." The door slid softly behind him and Jolie had lain awake, replaying all the wonderful moments over and over again until she fell asleep. Her dreams were all jumbled images of Thad and gifts and lights and mistletoe.

The sound of small feet running on the hardwood floors outside her room, accompanied by the squeals of delight, brought her to a sitting position. As much as she was disappointed that Thad was gone, she shared a certain excitement with Zak.

"He came! Santa came!"

Yes, he had.

Three times.

Jolie smothered a laugh. Diving for the bedside table, she placed the last remaining condom in the drawer before getting out of bed.

A quick shower later and she was dressed and making her way down the hall to the great room. Everyone was up already except for Kaylee and Evan. The fresh smell of coffee and baking filled the air along with the excited sounds of Zak, who had already torn open his Christmas stocking and was playing with the elastic-propelled airplane he'd found inside.

"Stockings first, then we eat, and afterward we'll open presents."

"Awww," Zak complained as he chased the plane to where it dropped after careening off a ceiling beam.

"No complaints, Zak," Simon admonished. "Those are the same rules as at our house."

The boy's shoulders slumped as he gazed longingly at the pile of gifts beneath the tree. Jolie had never seen so many gifts and she realized she'd left hers back in her room. She hurried back to retrieve them and then returned, phone in hand to take pictures. The huge tree with brightly wrapped parcels, all sitting in front of a picture window with snow-capped mountains in the background... It was so perfect it couldn't be real. And if she hadn't been here to experience it firsthand, she'd have thought the whole thing was faked for a Hallmark card.

She placed the small packages under the tree with the rest and took another bunch of pictures. The stockings were her favorite part, real wool socks all tacked to the mantel of the huge fireplace, filled to overflowing with gifts.

When she saw the stocking with her name stitched across the front, Jo thought she might burst with excitement. Her very first Christmas stocking.

"May I?" She turned to Gloria, holding the stocking as if it was the most precious thing in the world.

"Santa left it for you, didn't he?" Gloria grinned and Jolie took the stocking to the same couch she'd shared with Thad last night and opened it, slowly pulling out item by item: a huge candy cane, a bottle of lotion, a small box of chocolates, a scented candle, bubble bath.

Clad in Super Woman pajamas and her hair uncombed, Kaylee plopped down on the couch beside Jo. "Are you okay?" she asked.

"Yes, why?"

Kaylee touched Jo's cheek. "You're crying."

Shocked, she wiped the tears away. "Oh, God. I don't know what's come over me."

Kaylee didn't press the subject as she stifled a yawn just as Evan joined them, carrying their stockings. Jo gave them the couch and went to find Gloria to see if she could help. Gloria was in the kitchen with her father and Sage. To say the woman glowed was an understatement. She was alight with energy and excitement as she flitted about the kitchen, pulling stuff out of the oven, arranging everything on beautiful platters and laughing with her father and the other woman.

"Can I give you a hand?" Jolie asked from the door.

Gloria glanced up and Jo could tell she was about to wave her off but she said, "I insist."

With a shrug, Gloria said, "Okay, why don't you take these platters out to the table."

After carrying out dishes of fruit, baked goods, pancakes with bacon and eggs and toast—another delicious feast—everyone sat down to eat like one huge, happy family.

The only thing missing was Thaddeus.

He still hadn't arrived by the time they were all seated in the great room, Dillon passing out the presents.

"A tradition in my family is to take turns opening gifts," Evan said.

"Oh, no! That'll take forever." Zak threw his head back in agony.

"Why don't we let Zak open all of his presents first, then the rest of us can take turns?" Jolie suggested.

"Good idea," Dillon said.

The boy didn't even wait for his father's approval. He tore into the gifts, paper flying. Lego, a remote-controlled car, a Star Wars light saber, a cap and mittens—which got tossed aside as "boring"—a puzzle, some books—one of which was from Jolie, whom he grudgingly thanked—and finally, the highlight of the day was an iPod. Zak danced across the floor, his arm raised, shouting, "Thank you!" to Santa as if Jolly Old St. Nick could hear.

Simon ruffled his son's hair, smiling.

After cleaning up Zak's wrappings, the adults went around in a circle, opening gifts. Jolie had never received so many. She felt giddy and guilty all at the same time. Christmas wasn't supposed to be about the gifts, but she had to admit, exchanging presents was really fun. She'd loved shopping for everyone—even if Zak wasn't thrilled about his book. But opening up her gifts was just as exciting.

A knitted cap, scarf and gloves from Sage and Andy.

Some special soaps and bath products from Kaylee and Evan.

A beautiful picture frame from Gloria and Dillon.

She even received a pretty turquoise necklace from Dillon's mom.

Just when it appeared as if all the gifts had been opened—except for a small pile for Thad and Curtis—Gloria rushed off, calling over her shoulder, "There's one more. Just hold on." She returned a minute later, holding a small, narrow package and passed it to Dillon.

"What's this?" Dillon asked as he unwrapped the box and lifted the lid. With a frown, he withdrew a cigar. "I don't smoke."

"It's not for smoking, silly. It's a symbol."

"Of what?"

"Of the fact that you're going to be a daddy."

Dillon blinked, as if unable to comprehend what Gloria was saying.

"I'm three months. It's official."

All of a sudden, Dillon let out a whoop and picked Gloria up, swinging her around.

Gloria and Dillon's family—Colton and Catherine, Sage and Andy—all got up, taking turns hugging and congratulating the couple.

Everyone was so taken with the news that Jolie didn't hear the footsteps coming from down the hall until they were right behind her. She turned eagerly. It was only Curtis.

Alone.

Jo craned her neck, but there was no one else there. While this was probably the most wonderful, magical Christmas morning of her life, there was one thing missing.

Thad.

HE HADN'T BEEN avoiding the big house. Okay, maybe he had. But after playing hooky yesterday, he really did owe it to Curtis to take care of chores today. There was a bit of fence that needed fixing and a few other jobs. Not that they couldn't have waited, but...

Hell, who was he trying to kid? He'd been avoiding Jolie, been given express orders to stay away, and this time he was in agreement. Sort of. Things had heated up way too fast with that woman. Somehow, in the span of only a few days, she'd gotten under his skin. What kept him away was the notion that if Ms. Duval could have such an effect on him in only a few days, how would he feel after another week?

It was time to cool things down a bit, and the best way to do that was to steer clear, because if experience was any guide, all it took was being in her proximity and all logic flew out the window.

Dammit, it wasn't just that he didn't do long term and it wasn't that they came from completely different worlds. He had to keep things casual for legitimate reasons. His safety and hers.

Yet even now, Thad's fingers twitched with the thought of her soft, satiny skin. His mouth watered at the memory of the taste of her.

Jesus.

Apparently avoiding the woman did fuck all to get her out of his system.

Thad was just finishing up in the stable when Dillon came out, grinning like a fool.

"What's got into you?" he asked, feeling edgy.

"Only the fact that I'm going to be a daddy."

Thad stared for a second and then clapped the man on the back in a manly hug. Dillon was more of a friend than a boss. Shit. There was going to be a little Dillon running around. Or maybe a fiery little Gloria. Would he be here to see that?

"And the mother of my unborn child has got it into her head that we're going to go on a hayride in that big sleigh that hasn't been used in over a decade."

"Don't you worry. I'll take care of it," Thad told him. "You get back in there and enjoy the festivities."

"Honestly?" Dillon said, glancing back at the lit-up house. "I'd rather be out here right now. Don't get me wrong, it's nice, but..."

"But what?"

"I need a little fresh air, that's all."

"Why do you think I've been out here all day?"

It was true, sort of. When you were used to being outside all day, sitting around in a house could drive you stir-crazy. But that's not why he was out here. Not that Dillon needed to know that.

In silence, they hitched up Starlight and Buckshot, their two Clydesdales, to the sleigh. The horses pulled it to the front of the barn so the men could load a bunch of hay bales onto it for people to sit.

"You've been missed inside today," Dillon said, breaking the silence of the last half hour.

"That so?"

"Jolie's been watching the door like a hawk."

Shit.

"You avoiding her?"

Without looking up from what he was doing, Thad said, "I'm just following the advice of your little wife."

"My *little* wife isn't always right, you know."

He glanced Dillon's way.

"But don't tell her I said that."

The men chuckled. "So what is it exactly that you are saying?"

"I'm saying you should do whatever you like. As long as it's legal."

Thad averted his gaze. "You're the boss."

Once the sleigh was ready, Dillon went back inside to mobilize the guests. Jolie was one of the first ones out. She was wearing a red scarf and cap that matched the rosiness in her cheeks. And lips.

Lord, she was a sight for sore eyes, even more lovely in person than in memory, which made her too damned dangerous.

"You want to sit up here?" Thad called, patting the seat beside him at the front of the sleigh. "It's the best seat in the house."

"Thanks."

He gave her a hand and pulled her up, tucking a big woolen blanket around her legs once she was seated. While they waited for everyone else, Jolie asked the question that Thad knew was coming.

"Where were you all day?"

"Chores."

She was quiet for a while. Then, "I thought you were avoiding me." She turned to him. "Were you?"

"No," he lied. "I owed it to Curtis to give him the day off after disappearing yesterday."

She nodded like that made sense, but her expression remained blank, as if she didn't quite believe him, which she shouldn't.

That was the last chance they had to talk before everyone else piled onto the sleigh, laughing and chatting. As Thad drove them around the pond they sang "Jingle Bells" at the top of their lungs. After the second time around, Thad pulled the sleigh up to the back of the house.

"One more time!" Zak shouted, but everyone else had had enough and climbed down to go back into the house.

Jolie waited for them to leave. "You coming in for hot chocolate?" she asked.

He did not allow himself to glance at her mouth.

"Naw. Best get back."

She frowned. Worse, she wet her lips. It was impossible to avoid looking at her.

Temptress.

"Okay." She started toward the house, then stopped.

He pretended he didn't notice.

"I'll see you tomorrow?" It was a question.

"I'll see you when I see you."

INSTEAD OF HOT CHOCOLATE, Jolie went back to her room. She was not hurt. She was not let down. If Thad was blowing her off, so be it; it didn't matter to her. This was a fling. Nothing else.

Sinking onto the bed, Jo rubbed the spot between her brows. The only problem was, she did feel hurt. She did feel let down and she didn't know what to do about it. Removing her phone from her pocket, she discovered she'd missed a couple messages from home while out on the sleigh, and now she realized that she'd completely forgotten the time change back home. Her mother would already have left for work.

Going to sit down at the small desk, she called home anyway, speaking to her father for a few minutes, her journal open so she could doodle while she asked about the meal, about work, about whether they had plans for the New Year.

"Dad?" Jolie said before her dad passed the phone to her brother.

"Yes?"

"Merry Christmas."

He paused and then replied, "Merry Christmas to you, too."

For some reason, that simple sentence brought tears to her eyes. She managed to keep it all in check when her brother came on, distracting herself by writing Thad's name down on the journal page.

What the hell was wrong with him? Why was he pushing her away? She wasn't stupid; he'd purposefully been steering clear of her today. And then on the hayride, he'd barely spoken to her. She drew a question mark beside his name.

"So, Mom says you're working on a big story. Organized crime or something?"

"Yes." At this point it was just easier to keep up the facade than to try to come clean.

"Who does it involve?"

"I can't say. I'm sure you understand." *Please let this conversation be over.* She already felt bad enough.

"Do you need any contacts? You know I'm prosecuting a case right now."

"I heard."

Jolie absently circled Thad's name, her mind still on feeling ditched instead of listening to her brother.

"I can give you the name of someone to talk to at the FBI."

"Okay," Jolie said, hoping that by agreeing they could get past this topic. She wrote down the name and email in her journal as well as a website link for the FBI's organized crime page. Why she did it, she couldn't really say other than she was so far entrenched in the lie that it had almost become real—sort of like her claim that she could have a no-strings-attached affair.

Jolie heard voices outside of her door and her stomach flipped in the hopes it might be Thad.

"Listen, Jake, I've got to go."

"Okay. If you need help, just let me know." He paused. "I'm proud of you."

The phone clicked before she had the chance to reply.

12

The best souvenirs can't be bought in a store because
they are not things, they are experiences.

Jo Duval

THE VOICES OUTSIDE turned out to be Evan and Kaylee, not
Thad. Disappointed, Jolie sat down to write in her journal but for the first time this trip, the words didn't flow.
She gave up after ten minutes of flipping her pen against
the blank page. So, she opened her laptop and uploaded
the pictures into a file, drumming her fingers while she
waited, trying to figure out what she'd done wrong. That's
when her gaze landed on the package that was still sitting
on her desk. When Thad had declined to come in for hot
chocolate after the sleigh ride, she'd pulled the package
from under the tree and brought it back to her room.

Well, at the very least, she had a legitimate reason to go
on over to the bunkhouse and knock on his door.

Pulling on her parka and hat, Jolie tiptoed to the front
door because she heard voices still coming from the great
room and she didn't feel much like explaining where she
was going.

"Where you going?"

Jolie spun around from zipping up her boots to find
Gloria standing there, a mug of tea in hand.

She lifted the gift and said, "I didn't have a chance to

give this to Thad. I thought he might appreciate it, seeing as he missed all the Christmas fun."

Gloria's lips worked as if she was at war with herself, one part of her wanting to say something while another part told her to stay quiet. The first part won.

"He's a gigolo," she blurted.

"A what?"

"A Don Juan, a rake, a rogue…a player. Whatever you want to call a guy who is a man whore, that's Thad."

"A man whore?"

Gloria nodded. Then she came closer and grasped Jolie's hand. "I'm sorry. I know you like him, and I wanted to say something from the start, but he always interrupts me. I don't mean to be the one to burst your bubble, but…"

Jolie laughed. She couldn't help it. The names were just too hilarious. *Man whore* in particular.

"What's so funny?"

"Why does everyone assume I want to *marry* Thad? God. All I want is a bit of fun. Don Juan loving, Louisiana-style, sounds divine, if you ask me."

"Really?" Gloria asked.

"Of course."

"Shit."

"What?"

"I kind of told Thad—no, ordered him—to stay away today."

Jolie quirked a brow. "You did?"

"Maybe?" Suddenly Gloria burst into tears. Jolie had no idea why or what to do, so she wrapped her arms around her and patted her awkwardly until the redhead pulled away, blotting her eyes.

"Oh, my God! I don't know what's wrong with me. I'm *so* emotional."

"Could it be because you're pregnant?"

"I don't know. I've never been pregnant before." She took Jo's hands. "Anyway, I'm really sorry for interfering. I shouldn't have done that and—" Tears erupted again.

Dillon appeared—thank God—and led a blubbering Gloria away.

"Is this what pregnancy's like? Uncontrollable crying?" Gloria smacked Dillon on the arm. "What have you done to me?"

Jo opened and shut the door before she had a chance to hear Dillon's reply. Gloria had told him to stay away. Now it all made sense. With her head held high, she crossed the yard, rounded the barns until the bunkhouse was in sight.

When she heard the dogs approaching, she almost turned around. But they came at her calmly, Sue in the lead, followed closely by Humper. With his tongue lolling, he looked like he was wearing a big old goofy smile.

"Hey, you guys," Jolie said, patting Sue on the head with her mitten.

The animals escorted Jolie right to Thad's door and he opened it before she had a chance to knock.

"Ms. Jolie. What are you doing here?"

"Seeing as you've been absent from Christmas, I thought I'd drop by and give you your gift." Reaching into her jacket, she pulled out the wrapped package and handed it to him.

"You shouldn't have. I didn't get you anything."

"You didn't need to." She shrugged and stomped her feet because it was cold out, but apparently she wasn't getting an invitation inside. Yet.

"Well, thank you." He held up the gift. "That was very thoughtful." He went to shut the door and Jo shoved her foot in the way.

"Whatcha doing, Jolie?"

"Open the gift."

Thad unwrapped the package. It was a leather journal—a near replica of hers—and a pen.

"It's for your stories. You should write them down."

"Thank you. That's real nice."

"You've been avoiding me." Jo pressed on before he could try to shut the door again.

"No. I—"

"Liar."

That shut him up for all of two seconds, and then a change came over him. His face went blank. Gone were the laugh lines at the corners of his eyes, which she loved, and instead his face looked like it was carved out of stone. No expression; thin lips. He looked dangerous. And sexy as hell.

"I know that Gloria told you to stay away today."

A muscle ticked in his jaw. "She did," he admitted gruffly.

"She called you a man whore, you know."

"A what?"

"I know." Jolie moved her other leg inside, leaning against the door frame so Thad wouldn't be able to shut it on her. "But here's the thing I don't get. She asked you to stay away from me right from the beginning, didn't she?"

"Maybe."

Jolie inched inside a little farther. "And you never listened before. Why today?"

"C'mon, Jolie. You know why."

She shook her head. "No. I don't. Explain it to me."

"This isn't real." He indicated the space between them. "And I don't want you to get the wrong idea. Particularly not at this time of year."

Jolie threw her mittened hands in the air. "You, too?"

"Me, too, what?"

"What is it about me that seems to say I am incapable of having a casual no-strings-attached affair?"

Thad gave his head a half shake. For the first time since she'd met him, he had nothing to say.

"Do I have a billboard across my forehead or something? 'Jolie Duval, looking for Mr. Right to settle down with and have babies. All single men beware!' Is that it?"

When Thad just stared at her, blinking, she poked her mitten at his chest. "Tell me."

"You want the truth?"

"Yes."

"That's way too long for a billboard."

She scowled at him. "This isn't a joke."

"Okay, here's the truth." He grabbed her hand and held it tight. "I've known plenty of women in my day. I know the type that can have no-strings sex." He placed her hand on her own chest. "*You* are not one of them, sweetheart. Oh, you *think* you know what this is." He indicated the space between them again. "But when push comes to shove and it's time to say goodbye…" Thad paused as his gaze dropped to her mouth.

"You don't think I can say goodbye?"

He didn't answer.

Leaning close, she said, "You want to know what I think?"

The angle of his head said no. But he replied, "Go on."

"I think *you're* afraid of getting attached."

Thad made a face.

"I know it's going to end when I leave, but it's *you* who's making a big deal about it, not me."

"Jolie, listen—"

"No, *you* listen. If you don't want to continue, that's one thing. But don't avoid me. Don't make me feel like a fool. Be man enough to—"

She didn't get to finish.

Thad yanked her inside. He slammed the door with his foot and pressed Jolie up against it once it was closed.

"Be man enough to what?" he said through clenched teeth as he pinned her against the solid door.

Jolie gazed into his stormy blue eyes. "To say it, to my face." She bit down on her lower lip.

Thad grabbed her chin and ran his thumb roughly over the surface of her lip. "Don't do that." His voice was low and menacing.

"Do what?" She touched his thumb with the tip of her tongue.

He groaned before crushing her lips with his. Not one bit of that kiss was gentle and Jolie loved it. She loved it more when he prodded her mouth open with an insistent tongue, and when he released her arms to unzip her jacket and tug it from her shoulders. That gave her freedom to drop her mittens and tear off her cap, leaving her hair wild and free.

It was like she'd run a race, she was so out of breath, particularly when Thad reached down between them, past the hem of her sweater, and slid his hand up the inside of her thigh, cupping her through the thick tights she wore.

"Lord, you are hot down here." He squeezed and Jolie wriggled against his hand. "A regular furnace." He gripped her, tights and all, causing Jolie to throw her head back and suck in air. "You look so sweet, but then…" His hand twisted between her legs and Jolie dug her fingernails into Thad's shoulders, crying out with pleasure.

"There's a fire brewing inside of you, isn't there?" He eased up on the hold and slid his hand under her sweater, pushing her bra up so he could squeeze her flesh.

"Thad," she moaned.

He abraded his stubble deliciously against her cheek

before kissing her again while grinding his pelvis against hers. Holding on to his shoulders, she wrapped her legs around his waist, needing to open to him, needing to feel him as close as their clothes would allow.

"I'm glad we understand one another." His body ground exquisitely against hers.

"Just a fling," she panted against his cheek.

His fingers threaded through her hair and he tugged her head back. "A holiday fling." He kissed her neck, though it was more like licking and biting.

She blindly fumbled with the buttons on his shirt. Desperate. The man made her frantic in her desperation. Her blood ran in a frenzy through her veins, her hands shaking with the mad need to undress him. Quickly.

Now!

While her legs were still wrapped around his waist and her fingers fiddled with his buttons, Thad carried her, with long, sturdy strides, through the sitting area into his bedroom. No time for lights. Together they landed on his bed, rolling and grappling, tearing one moment at each other's clothes, the next minute at their own. Thad took the time to pull a condom out of his nightstand and roll it on so that when they came together in the dark they were skin to skin. He moved on top of her, parting her thighs with his, kissing her soundly, his mouth hot and wet with the same need that drove her to wrap her bare legs around his waist again.

This was what she'd been craving.

This was the gift she'd wanted from him. A connection. A physical, primal connection to another human being. And that's what she got. Every inch of Thad's muscled body felt right as he moved over her. Every inch of his breathtaking cock made her feel whole, as he moved inside of her. Every kiss, every bite, every scratch from his beard felt exactly like the thing she needed.

"I've never…" she began, wanting to explain that she'd never felt so close to anyone before. But she stopped herself, realizing that was exactly the kind of sentiment that Thad would see as a warning that she wouldn't be able to say goodbye.

"I've never…" She didn't finish what she was going to say, thank God. Though he wanted to finish the statement for her.

He had never acted this way with a woman before. Never been unable to control himself like this. One innocent—or not-so-innocent—nibble on her lip and he was undone.

The need to be with Jolie was so overpowering it defied reason and logic. And it made him do stupid shit.

But if she was adamant that she knew what this was, well, hell, he was powerless to stop her when she set out to seduce him. Didn't want to stop her.

No, Thad wanted to keep going and going, making love to her morning, noon and night. For as long as it lasted.

He propped her knees up, opening her wider, and leaned all of his weight onto her as he increased his pace, feeling wild with lust and need. Those gentle hands of hers gripped his shoulders with a strength he hadn't known she possessed, biting into his flesh in a heavenly way. The only thing he'd change right now was to be able to see her. He loved watching her face as she came. Loved how her large doe eyes glazed over with passion. Loved how her cheeks flushed and her gorgeous mouth parted, swollen from his kisses.

The image of her was so clear in his brain, however, that it was like he could see her hair spread across the pillow, her breath hitching, her beautiful breasts flush with his chest.

Thad grabbed her hip bones, the need mounting, coming from the backs of his knees and shooting up his legs and into his cock. It came with such force that he knew she could feel it, knew it from the gasp she made as his orgasm hit hard and fierce.

"Thad!" She grabbed his ass and held him there, trembling beneath him. That's when he realized her body was pulsing and vibrating around his.

Coordinated orgasm? No way. It was too good to be true. This *woman* was too good to be true.

Rolling over with Jolie in his arms, not wanting to let her go, Thad realized one very important thing.

Jolie had been right. It wasn't her he should be worried about. It was him.

He was the one who was fucked.

JOLIE SAT IN the lodge of Mystic Mountain Ski Resort, her laptop open on the table in front of her. She was drinking a big mug of hot chocolate with tasty peppermint schnapps and a dollop of whipped cream on top, pretending to work.

Except the whipped cream was distracting.

It made her think of Thad. Not that she'd ever seen him eat whipped cream, but she'd like to, preferably with him licking it off parts of her body. She squirmed in her seat, letting the lingering sensations from this morning settle over her.

Thad letting her sleep in while he left at some god-awful hour to do chores.

Then…slipping back into bed, freshly showered after chores, waking her up gently.

Being roused in the most scrumptious way possible,

with kisses, licks, caresses…a hard male body sliding over hers…into hers.

She shut her eyes to enjoy the memory.

It took a family of four clambering around the table beside her to pull her dirty mind from her lustful thoughts. She needed to get some work done, which was why she was here at the ski hill and not back at the ranch, lounging in bed with the sexiest man she'd ever met. She was on assignment and Jolie had to remind herself of that.

So she'd nearly broken her neck this morning, taking ski lessons with a bunch of four-year-olds. She'd vowed to try new things on this trip and she was proud of herself for doing it. But once the lessons were over, Jolie had beelined for the lodge, claiming she needed to work, while the rest of the party skied. She plugged her phone into her computer and uploaded the pictures from the day into the file folder for the *Travel America* article. Once the new images had transferred, she scrolled through all of her pictures, all three hundred seventy-five of them.

That was weird.

She surfed through them again.

How was it possible to take three hundred seventy-five pictures of the ranch and area and not get a single one of Thad? Well, when she got back to the ranch, that was the first thing she'd do. Get a whole bunch of pictures of him. She had no doubt he'd be photogenic, with those striking blue eyes and rugged good looks—the Marlboro Man, a billboard for the ranch. She'd have to get him to sign the waiver, of course, but an image of Thad would be as enticing as any of the other photos of the ranch. Maybe more for the female audience.

Something hot twisted in Jolie's gut at the thought of other women ogling him online. Maybe she should keep the pictures of him for her own purposes.

Using the free Wi-Fi in the lodge, Jolie typed *Thaddeus Knight* into a search engine and hit Return. Why hadn't she thought to do a search on him before?

Because you've been too busy having sex with him.

True, but it was never too late to look him up and ogle him online. Stalk him. See which sites he frequented. Learn a little more about the enigmatic Louisiana ranch hand.

Jo browsed the results of the search: there were links to Facebook pages, LinkedIn, Google images, articles… Plenty of people called Thaddeus Knight, but not *her* Thaddeus.

She added the term *Louisiana* and came up with more hits, but none were of Thad. She tried *Montana* and *Half Moon Creek*, but there was nothing there either. The man had no online presence whatsoever. Of course, he lived a simple life as a ranch hand; obviously he was one of the few remaining people who hadn't bought into the world of social media. And why would he?

Still…

Tapping her fingers against the tabletop, she figured getting pictures of him was now dire because she would absolutely need something to remember him by and clearly keeping in touch via social media was out of the question.

The hot mess in her gut twisted some more. With a hand to her temple, she chided herself. She still had a week to enjoy Thad's company. She'd worry about leaving later. For now, she needed to get to work on her *actual* assignment so that when she got back to the ranch she could work on the stuff she did for fun. Writing about Thad in her journal or, better yet, making love to Thad for real.

13

A picture may be worth a thousand words, but a thousand pictures is excessive.

Jo Duval

IT WAS RARE FOR Thad to fall asleep with a woman. If he did, it never happened twice. But here he was, for the third night in a row. One minute Jolie was giving him a recap of all the firsts from the trip: petting a canine, dogsledding, snowshoeing, cutting down a Christmas tree, opening a stocking, downhill skiing…the list went on and on. The next minute he was waking up at 5:00 a.m., his internal clock telling him it was time to get up for chores. Slowly and carefully, he eased his arm out from under her, trying not to rouse her.

Unfortunately, or fortunately—Thad couldn't quite decide—Jolie did rouse, and she sounded sexy as hell, making faint little sounds as she snuggled warmly against him.

"Where you going?" Her voice was so soft and sweet he grew hard just because it reminded him of other soft, incredibly sweet parts of her.

"Work."

"Oh." She sighed and fit herself right back into his arms.

Lord, all he wanted was to kiss her into wakefulness and make love to her all over again. But he needed to get up. He extricated himself and sat up on the edge of the bed.

One of her lovely hands snaked beneath the covers, finding his bare thigh and questing up higher. Thad was already sporting a morning woody, and her delicate hand only made the situation worse.

Or better.

"Don't do that, baby."

"Why?" she asked sleepily, stroking him. "This part of you seems to like it."

"More than likes it. But a man can't shirk his duties."

"You can't?"

"No, baby. I can't."

Her hand went slack around him. Dammit. With regret, he eased it off him and stood. "You go back to sleep. I'll be done in a couple of hours."

"Mmkay."

He leaned down to kiss her forehead and Thad was pretty sure she was asleep already. He dressed quickly, putting on the clothes from last night—the cattle didn't mind—and thinking once he was done, he'd shower and slide into bed, just like he had yesterday morning, and finish what they'd started.

Thank God the woman was leaving in less than a week because this was becoming dangerous.

Dangerously addictive.

JOLIE COULDN'T GO back to sleep after Thad left for chores. Her mind decided it wanted to replay the last few days over and over again. Skating on the pond and doing some simple jumps. Okay, so she was showing off. So what? Having another wonderful dinner in the big house, playing games. Then, when everyone else opted for a hot tub, she chose a hot shower…with Thad…in his bunkhouse.

She'd done things in the shower with Thad that she'd never tried before. Wonderful, naughty, sexy things.

Things she wanted to do again.

Now that the air had been cleared between them, everything was easy. Fun. Exciting. She'd been staying in the bunkhouse the last few nights because it was more private and cozy. Plus, it made it easier for him to get up and go to work, and he didn't have to sneak out in the middle of the night.

God, she could get used to this.

She rolled over in bed and checked the time on her phone. Six in the morning. Throwing off the covers, she stepped out into the cool morning air and found the overnight bag she'd remembered to bring with her this time. Staying here was less trouble for him but there was nothing like showing up at the lodge looking like hell warmed over. Or rather, like she'd been having monkey sex, which was the case.

Setting hairbrush and toothbrush aside for later use, she found her journal tucked into a side pocket. Because she'd been so busy skiing and Googling Thad and having fun and making love, she'd neglected to write in it yesterday, and she planned to make up for that, right now. Pictures of Thad were one thing, but her musings and stories would be an even better way to stay connected to him once she left. She reread the first few pages and was rewarded by a tightening of the rib cage.

It was going to be hard to leave. Worse would be the weeks that would follow.

Okay. So she'd lied her face off. Jolie Duval was not a fling kind of girl, no matter what she tried to tell Thad, or Gloria, or…herself. But it was too late to back out now. She was just going to enjoy it and deal with the pain after.

Crawling back into the bed, she fluffed some pillows behind her, plucking one from Thad's side of the bed and burying her face in it. She breathed deeply of his scent—

divine—before propping it on her knees as a makeshift writing desk.

She opened her journal and began to write. Some of what flowed from her fingertips was the truth, a recounting of their love affair; some of it was completely made up. In today's entry, Thad was a fugitive on the run, a man with a troubled past hiding out in Montana, and she was his captive.

A willing captive.

She rubbed her knees together, her imagination going wild. He'd kidnapped her and spirited her off to the old ghost town, because she knew too much and threatened to expose him. He meant to kill her but his desire for her was too overpowering. Finding themselves in close quarters, the attraction became too much for both of them and they ended up having wild kinky sex right there on the floor of the old hotel. She was just finishing up the scene when Jolie heard footsteps outside on the wooden stoop.

She quickly finished her thought and closed the journal, leaving it on the small nightstand. She was of half a mind to pretend to be asleep, because she longed to be "woken up" by Thad in the same way he'd roused her yesterday. However, the place was too small and she was too slow. Thad was already standing in the doorway, gazing in at her.

"Morning, sunshine."

"Morning."

"Did you sleep?"

She shook her head.

"Sorry about that."

"Don't be. I ended up getting some work done." Okay, maybe it wasn't work, *exactly*, but she'd been productive. She smiled as she let the covers drop, revealing the fact she wasn't wearing anything.

Thad leaned against the door frame, his stance casual, his gaze anything but. "I need a shower." His voice was gruff.

"So do I."

"Do you, now?"

"Yes."

"That's convenient because I happen to have one."

"Do you, now?" She repeated his phrase, doing her best imitation of a Southern drawl.

He stalked into the room and for a second, Jolie thought they might forgo the shower, because he stood beside the bed, his gaze sliding hotly over her bared breasts before settling on her face. "C'mon, then." He winked and turned toward the bathroom, shedding his clothes as he went.

Oh, yes, she could definitely get used to this.

IT WAS A beautiful day, the kind that made Thad glad he'd chosen Montana to hide. The sky was clear and appeared bluer because of all the fresh snow covering the ground and hanging heavy from the trees. The perfect day to take a group out snowshoeing. Apparently everyone staying at the ranch felt the same way, because the whole crew was there. Everyone except Curtis.

He'd willingly stayed back to do some tinkering with the front-end loader. It wasn't necessary work, but Curtis was a loner, even more so than Thad, and the man was probably glad to be back at the ranch on his own.

They'd all driven out as far as they could along the forestry road that led to Silverton. Once parked at a dead end, they suited up with the snowshoes the Crosses had rented for just this purpose.

"Eventually, I'd like to have our own," he overheard Gloria saying to Jolie as they started to make their way along a nearby trail. "Cross-country skis, too. We're thinking of building a ski shack on the other side of the pond and grooming our own trails. We've already got the snowmobiles, but the track setter wasn't in the cards this year, though that's the plan."

"You're running an amazing operation here," Jolie said reassuringly. "I can guarantee you'll be booked to capacity next winter after this article comes out."

Thad caught Gloria's eye and she smiled, giving him some kind of meaningful look. What the hell did that mean? The woman was hot then cold. Unlike Jolie, who was cold…then hot. He switched focus to the woman in question, ready to give her a suggestive wink.

His smile dropped.

She had her phone up in front of her face, taking his picture.

Oh, fuck, no.

He snowshoed closer. "Whatcha doing, Ms. Jolie?"

"The lighting is perfect." She smiled. Oh, she could get away with so damn much with that adorable smile, but pictures were one thing he could not allow.

"It is, isn't it?" He held his hand out for her phone. "Let me take some shots of you." He indicated behind her where a snow-covered peak rose majestically. "You need to be in your own article."

She handed the phone over and Thad made a show of taking a bunch of pictures from different angles. "How about the whole group now?"

Before taking the shot, Jolie explained to everyone that if she included the photo in her article, she'd need everyone's permission and they'd have to sign waivers. No surprise, everyone wanted to be in the shot. Who didn't want to be immortalized in print?

Thad, that's who. Which was why he was the one with the camera phone.

He took a bunch more shots, wanting to bury what he'd done.

"It's a fine day for pictures," he said, handing the phone back to Jo. "You should get lots of good ones today for the article." He hurried on, needing to distract her before she went scrolling through the images on her phone.

With Dillon in the lead, the group set out again and Thad made sure to keep Jolie in his sights. He couldn't afford another sneaky pic, not that he'd ever give her permission to use it, but just knowing there were pictures of him out there roaming around on someone's phone, computer, cyberspace. No way. Couldn't happen.

"This is a pretty different landscape from Louisiana, isn't it?"

"Yep," he said, feeling relieved when she tucked her phone away. "You ever been down there?"

"Just to New Orleans on spring break."

"You go crazy on Bourbon Street?" he asked gruffly.

"Not like my friends. I was too busy doing walking tours. You know—ghost tours, cemetery tours, plantation tours, that kind of thing."

He quirked a brow. "Touristy stuff?"

"Maybe, but better than wasting an entire trip at a bunch of cheesy voodoo bars, flashing strangers for cheap beads."

His gaze landed on her chest and the idea of his Jolie flashing any part of herself to some horny drunk made his gut burn.

"I loved the music, though."

"Yeah. Great music scene." He tried to imagine Jolie wandering around his hometown. It somehow made him feel closer to her, thinking that they'd walked the same streets, seen the same sights, maybe even been inside the same bars listening to music. Together. Only separated by time.

Sha, he was getting too philosophical for his own good. "You get your fortune read?"

She shook her head. "Nope." She sniffed, like it was a ridiculous question.

"What?"

"I don't believe in that stuff."

"You don't believe?" He stopped, letting Kaylee and Evan pass. Taking her hand, he removed her mitten and turned her palm up, gently flattening her hand and gazing at it as if reading a book.

"If you say I'm going to live a long and healthy life with lots of travel, I'm going to punch you."

Chuckling, he said, "I'm many things, but I'm not a charlatan." He traced the lines on her hand. "It's as simple as our life experiences getting imprinted in our skin, just as they do in our hearts and our souls."

She frowned up at him.

"Okay, this is your dominant hand, right?"

"Yes."

"So, the lines on this hand relate to the destiny you create. This—" he indicated the line between her thumb and index finger by following it "—is your life line."

"And what does that line say about my life?"

"You see where it's forked here? That means that you're surrounded by split or conflicting energies and your path will or already has been redirected."

She rolled her eyes.

"This one is your head line and let me just say, Ms. Jolie, yours is *very* interesting."

"Oh, brother. Why's that?"

"You see here where it's chained? That means you're conflicted and confused. And then down here it forks, this is called a writer's fork and means you're extremely creative and imaginative."

Her eyes narrowed. "You're using information you already know about me. That's called cheating."

Thad shook his head, leaned in and whispered, "The lines don't lie."

She shivered and Thad was certain it was not due to cold. "Now, I've saved the best until last. This..." He followed the line that ran beneath her fingers. "This is your heart line."

"Uh-huh? Pray tell, what does mine say? I'll meet a man named Thad and have wild, passionate, no-strings-attached sex. Then I'll leave brokenhearted and never love again?"

"Why, Ms. Jolie, you *do* read palms."

She tried to tug her hand free but he held on, running the tip of his finger lightly along the line again. "You've got the best heart line there is."

"Why's that?"

"It's long and curved, which means you're sensitive..." He grazed the backs of his fingers over her palm and she sucked in a breath. "Warm..." He took her hand and held it to his cheek. "Intuitive..." His gaze met hers, and then he curled her hand around his and kissed the backs of her knuckles gently. "And passionate."

Her chest rose and fell as she stared into his eyes.

"Though you may have a naive belief in happily-ever-after."

She yanked her hand out of his and pulled her mitten back on. "Where did you learn such nonsense?" She started walking again, following the trail of snowshoe prints. The rest of the group had moved beyond their line of sight.

"My grandmother had a shop in the French Quarter. She read palms—among other things—for a living."

"No way. And she could get by doing that?"

"Of course. She came from a long line of fortune tellers."

"I thought you said you were Cajun."

"I said I was a little of this and a little of that." He grinned as he caught up with her. "A purebred mongrel."

She smiled back. "You've never been back, huh?"

Shit. Thad realized too late how much he'd revealed. He'd never told anyone else about his grandmere. Never talked about life in NOLA. But with Jolie, it just came out, easy as anything.

"Naw. Nothing to go back for."

"You must miss it, though. And your grandmother? You must miss her."

A damn rock got lodged at the base of Thad's throat. It was a stone made of anger, guilt and shame, and he hurried on ahead, not wishing to continue the conversation and having no cooperating vocal cords to change it either. Thank God the group was gathered up ahead in a clearing.

"There you are," Dillon said. "We thought this would be a good place to build a *quinzee*."

"What's that?" Jolie asked curiously.

"The word is native Alaskan for *snow cave*," Thad supplied, removing his pack and issuing collapsible shovels to whoever wanted to help.

"Me, me, me!" Zak cried, being the first to grab one.

Jolie's eyes lit with interest. "So, how do you make it?"

"Pile up snow." He indicated the area. "Find straight sticks and stick them in all about the same distance around. Let the snow settle and then dig a cave."

"What are the sticks for?"

"They're a guide so you don't make the shell too thin or it'll collapse."

She beamed at him. "You really do know a lot about pretty much everything."

"I been around, Ms. Jolie. I been around."

"Hey, chatty," Colton called, dumping a shovelful of snow on Thad's feet. "You going to help or just flirt?"

After giving Jolie a kiss on the cheek, Thad joined the others, shoveling snow into a pile while Jolie went to help Gloria and Catherine find sticks of a suitable length.

It must have been twenty minutes later, when the pile was almost high enough, that Jolie called, "Hey, Thad?"

He glanced up.

"Smile."

She took his picture and another and another. After lowering the phone, she said, "That's for all the ones you deleted."

14

While a journal is a traveler's best friend, be careful
not to leave it lying around for prying eyes to find.

Jo Duval

JOLIE RELAXED AGAINST the edge of the hot tub. Two critical
differences this time around. First of all she was wearing
a bathing suit, which was important because, second, she
wasn't alone.

"Dad, can we make a *quinzee* at home? That was so
cool! We could even sleep in it. Thad said so."

Simon smiled. "Sure, Zak. We could do that."

Kaylee poked a toe out of the steaming water and
watched the steam roll off her foot into the cold night air.
"I don't know about the rest of you, but this has been the
best vacation." She turned to Evan, whose lap she was
basically sitting on, and said, "I had my doubts, but this
was a good call."

"I'm glad you're happy, babe."

Touching her forehead to his, Kaylee whispered, "The
best first Christmas ever."

Everyone had someone. A father, a son, a new husband.
What did she have? Jolie glanced at the empty seat beside
her. She had a holiday fling that was going to end in a few
days, that's what.

"You look awfully serious," Kaylee said, nudging Jo under the water.

"I was just thinking that this is the best Christmas holiday I've ever had, too."

The young woman grinned slyly. "It helps when you're in love."

"I'm not in love."

"No? In lust, then?"

"Dad, what's lust?"

Jolie blushed, though the heat from the tub probably covered it up.

"Sorry, I shouldn't tease you. Evan and I met on a vacation, too, you know."

"Really?"

"Yep. One of those ski trips." She turned back to her new husband. "Two years ago."

"Best years of my life."

Simon coughed. Whether it was to remind the newlyweds that a minor was present or because he was jaded about love, Jo couldn't tell.

Out of nowhere, a snow missile plopped into the tub, splashing everyone and making Zak squeal.

"Speak of the devil," Kaylee said, giving Jo a meaningful look.

Thad stood on the other side of the deck, another snowball poised in hand, ready to throw.

"You coming in?" Kaylee called, asking the question Jo had on the tip of her tongue.

"Naw. I gotta go get cleaned up. But y'all enjoy and maybe I'll surprise you again later."

"How you going to surprise us?" Zak asked eagerly. "Another snowball?"

"Son," Simon said quietly, "I don't think he was talking to you."

Just as Thad turned to walk away, Jolie leaned over the edge of the tub, grabbed a handful of snow from outside, formed a quick ball and chucked it at Thad's retreating back. It hit him square between the shoulder blades.

He slowly turned with an appreciative grin on his face. "Was that you, Ms. Jolie?"

"Maybe." She crossed her arms over her chest.

"Pretty good arm on ya."

Suppressing a grin with a twist of her lips, she said, "Thanks."

"For a girl."

THAD TOWELED HIMSELF off after stepping out of the shower. Seeing Jolie in the hot tub brought back all kinds of memories. Was it possible it was six days ago he'd first caught her in the raw? Holidays were like that, he supposed. The days just seemed to be jammed packed, so they seemed longer. It brought people close when every day was filled with excitement.

He glanced down at his own growing excitement. Jesus, Mary and Joseph, the mere thought of the woman aroused him. It'd been a long time since that had been the case. He dressed quickly before things got out of hand, and stretched out on the bed, waiting things out until he could go over there and sneak into the lovely Jolie's room.

Nothing made a man feel more like a randy teenager than sneaking into a woman's room. Thad chuckled. Not that the sneaking was really necessary anymore, but it sure was fun.

Would she be waiting for him naked again? He sure as hell hoped so.

Thad reached for the book on the nightstand, a thriller he'd picked up at the secondhand store in Half Moon

Creek, but instead of a book, his hand landed on the journal Jolie had given him for Christmas.

He opened the drawer of the nightstand and found the pen. Maybe he'd jot a few stories down while he waited.

At first Thad was confused when he opened the cover, because the journal was nearly full with feminine handwriting. Then he realized this wasn't *his* journal. It was hers.

A slow smile inched across his face as he flipped through the pages, skimming.

Stories. The woman was a storyteller. He flipped to the middle of the journal and then stopped when he saw his own name.

"Oh, Jolie, what did you write about me?"

"What did you say your name was?"

"Thaddeus Knight. At your service."

"You said you're a hand. What does that mean, exactly?"

"I could tell you, but showing you would be way more fun." His gaze swept over her body, his eyes dark with desire.

"Then you'd better show me."

"It'd be my pleasure."

She'd written the hot tub scene from the first night, only she'd embellished it.

"You're so beautiful. I wanted you from the moment I saw you."

"Kiss me."

He smiled before swooping in. His lips were hot and cold all at the same time, a wonderful combination as he nipped at her mouth before plunging his tongue inside. Under the water, he caressed her breasts, her stomach, his hand sliding down to between her legs.

"May I touch you here?" he asked against her lips.

A Southern gentleman.

Thad snorted and read on, the next three pages describing a very different outcome to her first night on the ranch. Thad could tell where she'd picked the story up the next day because there was a break on the page and it was a completely new scenario. They were still on the ranch but hadn't had sex. It was Tip's Eve and she was returning to her room...

The shadow of a man—a large man—stood by the sliding glass doors.

"What are you doing here?"

"What do you think?"

She wanted this, but she still felt a tinge of fear at his shadowy presence.

"If you don't want this, tell me now, and I'll go. But if I go, you can't look at me like you did earlier tonight."

"What do you mean?"

He crossed the room to stand right in front of her, gazing down at her. "No more licking your lips."

She licked her lips out of nervousness.

"No more dirty thoughts when you look at me."

She blinked.

"No more smiles, all innocent and seductive at the same time..."

Damn, the woman could write. It wasn't just a fantasy, it was a full-blown erotic story with him as the hero, and it was as arousing as if it was all happening in person. Thad adjusted the fierce erection throbbing behind his fly as he shifted on the bed to check the time. Would they be done the hot tub yet? Would she be showered and waiting in bed for him?

No. He should probably give her another half hour at least. So he went back to the journal, his blood pounding hotly through his veins and his cock stiffening painfully as he read her sexual fantasies, each one getting a little hotter, a little more bold. Handcuffs, rope, her teasing him, him teasing her.

He didn't even notice when he'd started rubbing himself through his jeans, and he popped the button about to unzip his fly when he turned the page and stopped.

Cold.

He stared wide-eyed at where his name—Thaddeus Knight—was traced in bold, circled over and over again, question marks bracketing it. To the right was a name, an email and a web address and beside that a chilling description.

FBI organized crime division.

Cautiously, he flipped the page. There was more but he only read the first few pages. This story was about a dangerous fugitive kidnapping a woman, holding her hostage and threatening to kill her.

Fuck.

JOLIE STOOD IN the mirror of the en suite bathroom, staring at her reflection. What did Thad see in her? Her face was sort of ordinary, her eyes a nondescript brown, her mouth too big. She frowned.

What did anyone see in another person? What made chemistry happen between two strangers? Take Kaylee and Evan. They met much like she and Thad had and now, two years later, they were married.

The weird thing about this trip was, even though Jolie had forced herself to do a bunch of stuff she'd never done before, and be a person she'd never been before, she actually felt more like herself than ever before. Life was weird.

Her phone rang from the other room and she wrapped a towel around her torso to retrieve it.

"Hey, Mom."

"Jo, I was hoping to hear from you. How are things going with the story?"

Was it her mother's question that irked her or the fact that the lie she'd told was still hanging over her? "You know, instead of asking about the story, you could ask about me."

"What?" As usual, her mother didn't sound hurt, she sounded confused.

"Mom, you haven't even wished me Merry Christmas."

"You know I don't use the word *Christmas.*"

"But I do." Jolie sat up straight on the edge of the bed. "I like Christmas. In fact, I've just had the best Christmas ever." She tugged on a thread on the comforter. "That's my story."

There was silence on the other end of the line. Jolie waited it out.

"I don't understand."

"I don't have some big story, Mom. I'm in Montana at a guest ranch, writing an article for *Travel America* on the best place to spend Christmas if you can't spend it at home."

"Why did you lie?"

"I don't know." Jolie pressed a hand to her forehead. "Maybe I was trying to impress you, which is stupid because I've never been able to impress you, so I don't know why I keep trying."

"What are you talking about?"

Jo sighed, hanging her head. "Only the fact that I'm the family failure, Mom."

"Excuse me?"

Really? Did she have to spell it out? Rubbing her brow, she said, "Everything you do is productive and important. Same with Dad and Jake. But me?"

"What about you?"

"My life has no meaning. I don't do anything important."

"Have I made you feel that, Jolie?"

"Yes. No. I don't know."

Her mother was silent, which was her typical response when she was preparing for an analysis. But that was not what Jolie got. Through the line came a sniffle and when her mother next spoke, her voice cracked with emotion. "I am so sorry if I've made you feel that way. But you need to know that you are not, and never have been, a failure to me or your father. Quite the opposite."

"But…"

"You're more of a mystery to us. A wonderful, delightful mystery. That means I might not understand where you're coming from sometimes—like this whole Christmas thing—but you've always been your own person. Strong. Creative." Her mother paused to blow her nose. "I am so proud of the woman you've become."

After the call, Jolie put on her nightshirt and climbed into bed. She lay in the semidarkness, blinking up at the wooden beams above her head. Could it be that she'd been wrong about her family's expectations of her after all these years? Did they truly admire her creativity, like her mother said? What if the only thing that had been holding her back from the life she wanted...was herself?

JOLIE ROLLED OVER in bed and groaned. Was it morning? How could it be morning when no one had come to her room last night? No one had slipped into bed and woken her up with kisses and caresses.

Still drowsy, she slipped her hands beneath her night-shirt and touched her body, imagining it was Thad, but she didn't get far before lucidity—or was it the smell of bacon and eggs from the dining room?—got her upright and out of bed. Well, she may not have had sex last night, but she'd sure slept well. Maybe it was the talk with her mother; maybe it was getting more than four hours of sleep, like she'd been existing on for the last few nights. Whatever the reason, Jolie felt like a new woman and she showered and dressed with a smile that was in direct contrast to her disappointment over Thad not showing up.

He probably fell asleep. If she was tired, he must be exhausted because he was the one up while it was still pitch-black, doing chores in the cold, taking care of the guests...and her.

She needed to do something to thank him and Jolie knew just what it was she wanted to do. By the time she got to the dining room, Simon and Zak had just finished and there was no sign of the other guests. Gloria was sitting at the table eating and flipping through a *Travel America* magazine. When she saw Jo, she quickly closed it but then smiled sheepishly, knowing she'd been caught.

Jo took the seat beside her and pointed to the magazine. "You should look up some of the places that are featured here and see how they're doing. You can gauge their popularity by the number of reviews on TripAdvisor and other sites."

With a sly grin, Gloria said, "I've already done it."

"And?"

"And having an article in this magazine is going to make a big difference to the ranch."

Jo covered Gloria's hand. "I have to tell you, I have had the absolute best time. Ever. This has been an amazing trip and you should be very proud of yourself."

Gloria crinkled her nose in delight. "That means so much." Her face grew serious. "And I'm sorry about how I was earlier. You know…about Thad." She sighed. "The truth is, he's good guy and I don't know what we'd do without him."

"Speaking of Thad…" Jo glanced over her shoulder to see if there was anyone in the vicinity before leaning closer and saying quietly, "Can you tell me if there's a place nearby where I can get lingerie?"

AFTER A SUCCESSFUL TRIP to Half Moon Creek, Jolie parked the car in the lot. She snagged the bag from Wanda's Women's Wear, a cute little shop in town that had everything from casual to formal clothes, Western wear, shoes, boots, accessories and lingerie. She glanced toward the barn and bunkhouse but didn't see any sign of Thad.

Her stomach growled. It was late afternoon and she'd considered stopping to grab a bite in town, but it had looked like snow and now she was glad she hadn't as snow swirled around her. She could hear the dogs barking out by the pond and the delighted shouts of a child. Zak was probably still out on the ice playing hockey with the crazy dogs.

Smiling to herself, Jo dropped the purchase off in her room before making her way down to the kitchen to grab something to eat. However, hushed voices from behind the closed door of the kitchen made her pause.

"What do you mean he's gone?" Dillon asked.

"I mean, he's not here." Though he rarely spoke, Curtis had an incredibly deep and distinctive voice.

"Is he with Jolie?" Dillon asked.

"No. She left to go to town a while ago," Gloria answered.

"You sure Thad didn't go with her?" her husband asked.

"Positive."

"When's the last time you saw him?" Dillon prodded.

"Last night," Curtis said. "He wasn't up for chores this morning, but I didn't think much of it, beyond annoyance."

"Maybe he just went to town for supplies."

"He's never done that before without telling me."

"No," Dillon said slowly. "Doesn't make sense since we stocked up the week before Christmas."

"Then there's the dogs," Curtis interjected.

"What about them?" Gloria asked.

"I don't think he fed them. Sue was scratching at the feed cupboard this afternoon."

"That doesn't sound like Thad," Gloria said. "Did he leave a note? A message?"

"Not that I saw. Truck's just gone."

"Anything? Any clue at all?"

"Yeah, one other thing. The rifle we keep in the barn is gone, too."

15

Just like you can be whoever you want when you travel, so can everyone else. Don't trust anyone.

Jo Duval

ALL THOUGHT OF HUNGER dissipated as Jolie quietly made her way back to her room. Thad was gone? Why? Was it something she'd done? Something she'd said?

She replayed the last time she'd seen him. It was while she was in the hot tub with everyone else. He'd seemed totally normal—joking, throwing snowballs and making a suggestive comment about visiting. That was it.

Normal.

Except now he was gone without telling anyone. Without saying goodbye.

Something was wrong, Jolie felt it in her bones, and she was going to find out what it was. Pulling on her parka and boots, she made her way across the yard, past the barn to the bunkhouse. Humper and Digger ran up to greet her, but Sue didn't. Jolie found her on the stoop of the bunkhouse, her head on her forepaws, looking forlorn. Her gut twisted as she bent down to give Sue a pat.

She tried the knob and the door opened. No surprise. She'd never seen Thad use a key to open the door before. The late-afternoon sun lit the sitting area and even though Jolie had spent the night here three times and had stayed inside without Thad, she felt like she was breaking and entering.

Everything looked much like it had the last time she'd been there: neat and sparse. The well-worn couch covered with throws, the cast-iron stove, with wood stacked beside it, the computer sitting on the small table that separated the kitchenette from the sitting area, the lamp, the shelf with books.

She wandered into the kitchenette and touched the bottom of the sink.

Dry.

She opened the bar-sized fridge to check the contents. Eggs, milk, cheese, beer, butter, some jars with jam and condiments. Nothing unusual.

Slowly, she made her way to the bedroom and switched on the light. The bed was made and everything was put away. Neat. There was nothing on the chest of drawers. Nothing hanging on any of the three hooks beside the door. It felt…empty.

Same thing in the bathroom. Not that she'd really paid much attention because she'd been in there with Thad, showering, which meant she'd paid plenty of attention to his bare chest, to his powerful shoulders and kissable lips, not to mention his lovely erection. She'd barely noticed the contents of his bathroom, other than to note he kept it neat.

She ran a finger along the bottom of the sink. It was dry, too.

Then she noticed his toothbrush was missing from the holder. She opened the drawer in the vanity. It was empty.

He was gone, and not just to town. The whole place felt…abandoned.

What the hell?

Her heart thudded behind her breastbone; she didn't know whether to be worried or broken.

"Ouch." Jo stepped on something. She knelt down to see what it was, only to find her journal on the floor, sticking out from under the bed. What was it doing there?

Oh. She'd been writing in it and must have left it on the night table. When was that? Yesterday?

So, why was it on the floor?

Had Thad read it?

She opened it, flipping through the pages and reading snippets of her entries, trying to see them through his eyes.

"I wanted you from the moment I saw you…"

"You're the most beautiful woman I've ever met, I don't know what I did before I met you…"

"Take your clothes off for me, nice and slow, and I promise I won't kill you…"

Oh, God! No wonder he ran. He was running from *her*. Could she blame him? Over and over she'd insisted this was only a fling and she wasn't becoming emotionally involved when all along she'd been writing crazy shit about him, the kind of ridiculous stuff that would make any red-blooded male run for the hills.

She covered her face. Should she tell Gloria what happened? Reassure her that Thad would be back once she left? In a daze of humiliation, she stumbled back through the sitting room and went to the door to put on her boots. However, just as she was bending over to pull her second boot on, something jarred her memory. She stopped what she was doing to turn around. Something was different about the room, something other than the fact that Thad wasn't there.

She surveyed the contents one more time, her gaze landing on the laptop on the table. And, what was that beside it? A cell phone?

Thad had a laptop and a cell phone? She'd never seen him use either, and they certainly hadn't been there yesterday morning when she'd left; she was sure of it. With one boot on and one boot off, she sat down at the little table and started up the computer, tsking when it opened without even being password protected. Clicking the search engine on the desktop, she opened up his browsing history, hoping it might give her some idea where he'd gone. Maybe he'd booked a hotel in Half Moon Creek or Butte. Maybe he decided to take a last-minute vacation—away from her.

She clicked on the most recent link and her confused heart exploded into a million pieces before settling at the pit of her stomach.

She was staring at the FBI's Most Wanted page—more specifically, at a picture of Thad. The man in the photo was much younger—barely more than a teenager—and his name was not Thaddeus Knight, but Lukas Hunter. Didn't matter the name; it was Thad. The striking blue eyes were a dead giveaway.

Lukas Hunter is wanted for his alleged involvement in the murders of three men in New Orleans on August 17, 2005. The men died of multiple gunshot wounds.

Hunter is approximately six foot two with dark hair and blue eyes. He has ties to Louisiana, Texas, Mississippi and Florida, and it is suspected that he may have fled to Mexico. He is a known member of the Salvatori crime family and is considered extremely dangerous.

Jo's lungs stopped working. She opened her mouth, but air refused to enter. Her pulse crashed between her temples and the little bits of her heart beat erratically from somewhere deep in her gut.

It couldn't be true. Thad was not a killer. He was not dangerous. This was a joke. A cruel, stupid prank.

She stared so long at the screen that her vision became blurry. Then she noticed the *drip*, *drip*, *drip* of tears on the keyboard.

"No." She stood up and paced back and forth across the small space. "No, it's not true."

But then...

Thad had no family, no attachments. He told plenty of stories but few about himself or his past. Did that make him a murderer? There was only one way to find out. She had to call the hotline number. Taking a deep breath, she reached for her cell phone in her pocket, having to input her passcode three times because her shaking hands kept missing. Not trusting her vision, she zoomed in on the computer screen to enlarge the print and typed in the 1-800 number. The phone rang five times before there was a click followed by silence. She tried the number again and the same thing happened.

Shit.

She set the phone down and reread the webpage again, determined to find something to indicate that she'd lost her mind and this was all some stupid mistake.

Her phone rang, and she jumped, the bits of her heart flying up into her throat.

"This is the FBI, did you make a call to our hotline?"

"Y-yes."

"You have information about the whereabouts of Lukas Hunter?"

Jo didn't answer.

"Hello?"

Everything was happening too fast. "I don't know."

"You don't know? Did you or did you not call this line?"

"I did. But I don't know if the person you're looking

for is the person I know." Jolie rubbed her brow. This was a mistake.

"That's for us to decide. Does the individual you know go by Lukas Hunter?"

"No. Thaddeus Knight."

"It's not unusual to use an alias. Does he fit the description on the website?"

"Sort of, but it was a long time ago and I can't be sure." Except that she was sure. She knew, beyond a doubt, she was looking at a younger version of Thad.

"Do you have a picture?"

"Yes," she said softly. "I do."

"Send it to us." They gave her an address to email the picture.

She scrolled through the photos on her phone until she came to the one of Thad. Her heart hammered in her throat as she gazed at it. A faraway voice called "Hello" from her phone and she typed in the email address, double-checking it before sending.

"Did you get it?"

There was a couple of seconds before she heard, "Yes. That looks like him. How close are you?"

"What do you mean?"

"Are you intimately involved?"

"What kind of question is that?"

"Lukas Hunter has a distinguishing mark on his shoulder."

Jo blinked. "What kind of mark?"

"A gunshot wound."

The phone slipped from Jo's slack fingers. There was no longer any doubt.

"Merry Christmas, Jolie," she whispered to herself. "You've been sleeping with a killer."

THAD FINISHED THE SOUP and put away his now-cooled camping stove, packing it beside the rolled-up sleeping bag in the backpack. He'd needed to be ready to run at a moment's notice, which was why he kept his bag with him at all times. It'd been stashed at the back of his closet for an occasion just like this. He hoisted it onto his back, then buckled his snowshoes and started walking again, making sure the spruce branch was secured and covering his tracks as he went.

The day was overcast; it smelled like snow.

Perfect.

Thad stopped and stared up at the gray sky. He'd gotten too comfortable at the ranch, and comfort had turned to recklessness. Eleven years was a long time to stay vigilant, but look what happened when he didn't. Jolie's face flitted across his imagination. The only nonessential item he had brought with him was the journal Jolie had given him. He didn't know why he'd packed that at the very last second. In his mind he could see her face, the light in her brown eyes, her beautiful mouth...her smile.

"Was she worth it?" he asked the sky, which replied by dropping big flakes of snow on his upturned face.

The truth of the matter was, he didn't regret what happened between him and Jolie. What he regretted was continuing to stay on at the Silver Tree after Dillon and Gloria had turned it into a guest ranch. All those strangers coming week after week? It was an invitation for trouble. If Jolie hadn't ratted him out, then someone else would have. What he didn't get was how she had been able to stay with him after she knew. Was she playing him like Raina had?

How could he tell? He'd been thinking with his dick ever since she arrived. Kind of like he'd done with Raina Salvatori. He wondered when Jo had figured everything out. Had she called the number right away? If she had,

they would have come for him already. But if she knew…
why hadn't they come?

Maybe he should have played it cooler, made up some
story about needing to return to Louisiana, but he'd panicked when he'd seen that journal. He'd taken care of what
he needed to and left in the middle of the night. There was
no turning back now.

Thad turned his gaze north. He'd cross the border in a
week, maybe two. With Canadian ID, he'd find another
ranching job. Though he'd have to work on his accent, because he was pretty sure Canadians didn't drawl. Maybe
he'd pretend he was Curtis, the strong, silent type. Keep
his pants zipped and his mouth shut, because he'd learned
the hard way that the only thing women and talking ever
did was get him into trouble.

JOLIE DIDN'T SLEEP a wink. She lay in bed all night, tossing
and turning, replaying every moment with Thad over and
over in her head, trying to reconcile the man she knew
with the man on the FBI's Most Wanted website. But she
couldn't. No matter how much her brain tried to tell her it
was true, her heart would not accept it.

A man can't shirk his duties…

*I'll tell you a secret about Santa, but you've got to prom-
ise not to tell anyone else…*

*Singing's good for the soul, you know. Connects us to
each other and to the angels…*

Not the kinds of things a hardened criminal would say
or do.

But maybe that's how dangerous individuals—the Dah-
mers and Bundys of the world—got away with stuff, by
being charismatic and adept at fooling people so that no
one would guess they were cold-blooded killers.

She turned on the light beside the bed and opened her journal, reading the entire thing through.

When she got to her last entry, she read it twice because she'd written about Thad being a fugitive.

Had some part of her psyche suspected the truth?

By six in the morning, she gave up trying to sleep and padded her way into the kitchen to make coffee. Gloria was already there, looking like she'd slept as much as Jo. When Gloria saw her standing in the entrance, she walked up and threw her arms around Jolie.

"I still can't believe it." It was the same thing she'd said over and over yesterday when Jolie had told them.

"I know."

Gloria pulled back. "How are you holding up?"

"About the same as you, I imagine."

Gloria wiped the tears from her cheeks. "Dillon and I talked about it. We're not going to tell anyone. Colton and Catherine left this morning, and everyone else is here through New Year's. When the FBI arrive later, we'll pretend they're regular guests, here for the New Year's Eve party."

Jo nodded.

With a sympathetic tilt to her head, Gloria said, "We'd totally understand if this is too much for you and you want to leave and go back to Chicago."

"I can't do that."

The other woman took her hand and squeezed. "Why not?"

Jo laughed without humor. "This is my big story. The one I've wanted since becoming a journalist. There's no way I can leave."

The rest of the morning was spent in a blur of pretending. How could the other guests not know what was going on when everyone was acting so weird? Particularly when

Zak asked where Thad was because he had promised to take him on the dogsled.

"He had an emergency with a relative back home. He had to leave," Gloria explained.

"Awww." Zak pouted.

Jolie had to look away because it was too painful. The memory of dogsledding; of Thad getting her to pet Sue. The memory of their first kiss, and the many kisses afterward—his mouth, his tongue, his strong, powerful muscles...

His gunshot wound.

"Our new guests have arrived," Gloria said brightly. Too brightly. But no one seemed to notice as Kaylee was curled up on the couch reading while Evan fed the fire and Simon tried to coerce Zak into a game of checkers.

"I was going to give them a tour," Gloria said in an overly loud voice, her gaze flitting around the room erratically. "Jo, would you mind coming with me? Maybe you'd like to interview them for your article."

"Okay," she answered in the same loud tone that Gloria had used.

Kaylee glanced up from her book and gave her a look. What was that, suspicion?

The other woman tilted her head to one side and semi-smiled.

Oh.

That wasn't suspicion. Kaylee felt sorry for her because Thad had abandoned her.

If she only knew.

16

In the event that you have to deal with the authorities while on vacation, be as helpful as possible.

Jo Duval

JO HURRIED BY ON her way to the foyer to put her coat and boots on. Once outside, she saw the black sedan—did all agents drive black sedans?—and the two individuals in long coats standing outside talking to Curtis and Dillon. Suddenly everything became real. Very real.

"Come on." Gloria linked her arm through Jo's and together they walked across the parking area to meet the FBI agents.

When they reached the side of the barn where the men were standing, Dillon turned to greet them. His face was serious and his voice deep. "Agents Ross and Edwards, this is my wife, Gloria and this is Jolie Duval, a guest staying at the ranch."

"Which one of you called?" Edwards, the bigger of the two agents, asked. He looked to be in his midthirties, tall and broad, his forehead wide, with bushy eyebrows shadowing an expressionless face.

"I did," Jolie said, stepping forward.

The other man closed the distance. He was older, late forties. He looked like he'd been around the block a few times and had seen a lot of shit that made him hard and cynical. "Thank you for calling," he said cordially, which surprised her because his stance was like that of a pit bull ready to fight.

"I didn't know what else to do."

"How did you know to call?"

She briefly explained how she'd gone into his bunkhouse after Thad had left, looking for some sign from him, when she'd found his computer and searched his browsing history.

"What do you think made him run off?" Ross asked.

Jolie shrugged. There was no way in hell she was showing the FBI her notebook. Uh-uh.

Thank God Zak and Simon chose that moment to come outside and head their way, because it saved Jolie from having to lie.

"What's up with the dogs?" Zak asked Gloria.

Jo had wondered the same thing as a cacophony of yips and howls echoed from behind the barn doors.

"Oh, they went a little nuts when the agen—new guests arrived. So we shut them up in the barn. They aren't happy."

"They miss Thad," Jolie said quietly, to which Gloria responded with a look of regret.

"Why don't you take them out for a skate?" Gloria said to the boy, pointing to the pond.

After Zak scampered off, Dillon said, "Let's continue this discussion in Thad's bunkhouse."

The group made their way over and went inside. The space felt too small for the six of them.

"Well, I'll say one thing for the man," Ross said as he took in the room. "This was a clever cover." He nudged Edwards. "I doubt his friends back in NOLA would believe this if they saw it."

"Why's that?" Jolie asked.

"Lukas was engaged to Raina Salvatori, the daughter of Gordo Salvatori, one of the wealthiest men in New Orleans."

"He had it all, until he fucked up," Edwards said.

"Yep. Three undercovers. What a fucking idiot."

"He killed police?" Gloria asked, wide-eyed.

"Allegedly," Edwards said with a wink.

"So, it hasn't been proven?" Jolie asked, a glimmer of hope taking root in her heart.

"Proven? Hell. What's there to prove? No one goes into hiding for eleven years if they didn't do it."

THAD SET HIS pack up against the entrance of the snow cave, blocking out the cold. He unrolled his sleeping mat and bag to rest. It was early afternoon, but the best thing to do was to stay under cover during the day and travel at night. This time of year was perfect because the days were so short and the nights so long.

He tried to sleep—it shouldn't have been a problem, because it was pitch-black inside of the cave and he hadn't slept last night, putting as much distance between him and the ranch as possible—but he couldn't. Switching on the flashlight, he found a candle and matches in the side pocket of his pack. Creating a little ledge, he swiveled the butt of the candle into the snow so it was standing upright and lit it. From another pocket, he pulled out the journal Jolie had given him and a pen that came with it.

The pen had a saying: a story only comes alive when it is shared. How true that was. As melodramatic as it sounded, if he was to die out here, he wanted to leave behind the true account of what happened in New Orleans. At the moment, he, Lukas Hunter, was the only one in the world who knew the truth.

The problem was where to start. He tapped the pen against the blank page, thinking.

A face materialized in his mind's eye. Dark, glossy hair, smooth skin, bow lips, long lashes. The face of an angel. The body of a siren. The conscience of a psychopath.

I met Raina Salvatori at the Pontchartrain Country Club when I worked there in the summer of 2001. It was lust at first sight, pure and simple. Oh, I thought it was love—what seventeen-year-old kid doesn't love with their dick when they're that age? She was beautiful, rich, sexy. One look, one touch, one secret kiss and I was hers to do with as she would. Yep. Lust consumed me. Blinded me.

She was my first and she told me I was hers, too. Now I know better. When I was twenty-one and asked her to marry me, she introduced me to her family, because she said she couldn't marry me unless they approved. I was so fucking naive. I knew the Salvatoris. Who in NOLA didn't know them? They owned half of the city—the rotten half. And then some. They're as crooked as a broken backbone. Grandmere warned me to stay away, but sex is a powerful thing, particularly for a horny kid. So when her father took me aside and asked me to prove how much I loved his daughter, I didn't even think twice. I shook that man's hand and told him I'd do whatever it took.

What a stupid fucking move that was.

ALL HOPE THAT Thad might be innocent deserted Jolie. The agents were right. Innocent people did not flee. They did not change their names and go into hiding for over a decade. She pointed to the table. "I'd never seen this computer before yesterday. Cell phone either."

She hadn't turned the computer off, so once they tapped the touch pad, the Wanted page popped up. They glanced at one another.

"Thad had a cell phone?" Gloria asked. She turned to Dillon and Curtis. "You ever see him use it?"

Curtis shook his head.

"No." Dillon reached for it but Edwards stopped him.

"Don't touch it."

"Why?"

"It's evidence. We'll take it." Removing gloves from the inside pocket of his jacket, Edwards picked it up and turned it in his hand as if needing to make sure it really was a phone and not an explosive device.

"Who do we have who can crack a password?" he asked Ross.

"Mikey?"

"No time."

"Try one, two, three, four," Jo offered.

They turned to her and frowned, as if she was eavesdropping, even though she was standing right there.

She shrugged. "The computer wasn't password protected. Maybe he just left the store settings on the phone, too. The password is always one, two, three, four. Right?"

Ross narrowed his eyes at Jolie before nodding for Edwards to go ahead and give it a try.

He had to take off his glove to work the touch screen, but the fact that Jolie was right was written all over his face after he'd tapped in the code. When he met her gaze, he said grudgingly, "Pretty smart."

He glanced at Ross, who gestured vaguely with his head. Edwards nodded, shoving the phone into his pocket. The agents spent a few more minutes searching the contents of the computer, but after not finding much of anything, they turned their focus to Thad's bunkhouse. They tore it apart, looking for who the hell knew what. Jolie couldn't watch as they went through the bedroom, opening up the drawer on the nightstand and raising their brows and snickering at the boxes of condoms tucked inside.

Gloria stood beside her, rubbing her back.

"Do the local police know what's going on?" Dillon asked. "Should we tell our other guests? Maybe everyone should go home."

Ross turned around and with a stern look said, "The answer to your first question is yes, we've alerted the police to our presence."

"And told them to stay away," Edwards interjected.

"Why?" Dillon asked.

"It's our case, our jurisdiction," Ross said. "And our experience is that the locals always fuck it up. If we need their help, we'll ask for it. Not the other way around."

Dillon frowned and glanced at his wife.

"The answer to your second question," Ross said in a patronizing voice, "is no. No one leaves. Not until we know what's what. Understood?"

"Is this going to be all over the news?" Gloria asked, her cheeks rosy and her hands clenched tightly in front of her. "You know, media coming out here and invading the ranch? Road closures? Nonstop TV coverage?"

Jo couldn't tell if this idea made Gloria excited or nervous. Probably both.

"No. This isn't the movies, Mrs. Cross. If we put everyone on high alert, we'll never see Lukas again. We need him to believe he's not being tracked. We need him to get careless, otherwise he's gone."

Edwards nodded. "Now, if any of you have any information, you tell us directly. Not the local sheriff, even if he is a friend of yours. *We're* your contact, got it?"

"In fact, it's a federal offense for you to share information with anyone else," Ross added, glancing meaningfully at Edwards.

"That's right," the other agent agreed.

"O…kay," Dillon said, a small frown tugging on his lips.

"You." Edwards pointed at Jo. "We need to talk to you. One-on-one."

"What about the rest of us?" Gloria asked. "We've known Thad for years."

"We'll sit down with each of you later. But for now?" He indicated the door with his head. "Leave."

Once the door shut behind the other three, Edwards pulled out the chair for Jo. The men did not sit, however. Oh, no, they stayed standing, leaning against the table, towering over her.

Ross rapped his knuckles against the tabletop. The action meant to startle her. "Tell us everything you know about Lukas Hunter, aka Thaddeus Knight, and don't leave out one fucking detail."

THAD COULD NOT believe his luck, or lack thereof. He'd turned his back on the food sack for two minutes to roll up the sleeping bag and pad, and a badger had stolen it. Or most of it, anyway. He bent to pick up the packets that had spilled out. The opened bag of seeds was probably what had attracted the critter in the first place. He could have shot the thing, too—he was that close—but a rifle shot would be heard from miles away and Thad couldn't take the chance.

Discovery or food. It wasn't much of a decision.

The last time he'd been put in that kind of position—shoot

or be shot—he'd made the same decision, and he'd do the same thing all over again.

The problem was, he'd lost a week and a half's worth of dried food and seeds. While he wasn't half bad at snaring, that wasn't going to suffice. He needed food to carry. Where the hell was he going to get that out here? He couldn't very well stroll into the nearest town and pop into the local grocery. Taking the map out of his pack, he sat in the snow and traced the route he'd intended—far away from all habitation. Nothing.

With his finger, he drew a line south of where he figured he was. Silverton. He absently tapped the dot on the map, thoughts of his visit there with Jolie invading his mind: kissing her, reaching up under her parka, making love to her for the first time after they returned...

No.

No more thoughts of Jolie. He had to focus on survival, not on the wonders of Jolie's killer mouth and sweetly seductive nature.

Focusing on the map again, Thad figured Silverton was about seven miles back, in exactly the wrong direction. But then, how far would he get if he just kept going? Damn, he wished he'd taken one of the snowmobiles from the ranch, but then they'd have known for sure what he was up to.

No, he had to trust that if they were looking for him— and his gut told him they were—then they were still off on a wild goose chase. Only an idiot would stay close to the ranch. Or an idiot who'd had his food stolen by a badger thief. No time to worry about that now. It was the middle of the day, not exactly the best time to travel, but he didn't have much choice. A man had to do what a man had to do.

JOLIE SAT AT the desk in her room, staring out at the late-afternoon sky. At least the tears had dried up, but now she just felt hollow. When her phone rang, she frowned, picking it up as if she didn't know what it was or what to do with it.

"Hello?"

"Hey, Jo. It's me."

"Oh, hey, Jacob."

"You okay?"

"Not really."

"I'm sorry. I had no idea this stuff was so important to you."

"Of course it is." How could finding out your lover was a hardened criminal *not* be important to her? Seriously. Her family really needed a crash course on emotions. "How'd you find out?"

"I talked to Mom."

Jo frowned. "How did Mom know?"

Jacob cleared his throat.

"Uh…you told her? You know, I get it. I do. People love Christmas and maybe spending it with strangers gives you a different perspective on things. You were always more creative and carefree than the rest of us. At first I didn't get why you lied, but…"

Oh, God. Jolie gave her head a shake. She and her brother were on *totally* different pages.

"…then I remembered something."

"What?" she asked automatically, even though she was barely listening.

"Remember when we went to Wisconsin to visit Dad's side of the family? God, you were so excited. I was, too. But you? It was like we were on our way to Disneyland. Anyway, Dad's family was a gong show—all a bunch of drunks. I don't think you saw it, though. You were too taken with the tree and presents and stockings.

"What you don't know is that Granddad was an ass,

bad-mouthing Mom, calling her names. I think that was it for Dad. Mom might not be all touchy-feely. She might not like big celebrations because she's uncomfortable in social settings, but she's strong and she's stable. She's everything Dad's family wasn't. And that counts for… Jo?"

"Huh?"

"Are you there?" he asked.

"Yep."

He sighed. "Is any of this making sense?"

"Sure."

He waited. "Okay. Something's off. What's really going on?"

Jo rubbed her forehead. "You know that big story I lied about?"

"The one about organized crime?"

"Yeah, well, here's the crazy thing. It's actually true."

"Jesus, Jo. Give it a rest. You don't need to try to impress me. I don't care that—"

"Jake. I'm not lying this time. I swear." Jolie gave her brother the five-minute version of what happened between her and Thad and how he disappeared, what she found on his computer and how she called the FBI.

Her brother was silent for a few moments. Then he said quietly, "Shit. This is serious. You need to get out of there because you do not want to be messing with these kinds of people."

"I have to stay."

"No, you don't."

"This is my chance," she insisted. "My big story."

"I told you, you don't need to prove anything to us. You're great just the way you are." It was probably the nicest thing her brother had ever said to her.

"But I need to do it for me." Her throat closed up, because it was true. She felt like a failure, not because her family made her feel that way, but because she was the one who compared herself to them and their success. She was the one who told herself she didn't measure up.

She wasn't going to do that anymore.

As painful as Thad's criminal past was, the big break she'd been searching for was staring her in the face. This sort of opportunity only came around once in a lifetime and she wasn't about to screw it up.

"Listen to me," Jake said urgently. "You are too close for this. If this guy is who you say he is, he'll play you as a pawn. That's what they do. I see these assholes all the time. They have no conscience and no concern for anyone but themselves. You're not safe."

"I can handle it, Jake."

He muttered something beneath his breath before exhaling heavily. "It doesn't matter what I say, does it? You always do whatever you want anyway, but at least tell me who you're working with from the agency."

"Ross and Edwards."

"Who?"

She repeated the names.

"Hmm. I don't know them."

"Yeah, well…" Jo realized that she wasn't supposed to be discussing the case as her ears picked up the sound of heavy footfall approaching her door. "Look, Jake. I gotta go. I'll call you later."

"Be careful."

17

In the event that the authorities are arrogant bastards,
you should still cooperate. Mostly.

Jo Duval

SHE ENDED THE CALL to her brother just as someone pounded
on the door, giving her only two seconds before opening
it without her permission and entering.

"The phone was a decoy," Ross said by way of greeting.

"Okay," Jo said, slowly rising to her feet.

"Did you know?"

"Did I know what?"

"It was left on purpose. To mislead us." Ross ran a
tongue along his top teeth. His expression was suspicious.

"I don't know anything about that."

"No?" Edwards asked, stepping forward.

"No."

"See, Lukas booked a bunch of tickets—planes and
buses going in all directions. We're watching them all
but I don't think he's on any of them," Ross said, striding
right up to her. "In fact, if I was a betting man, I'd wager
he hasn't gone anywhere."

"What do you mean?" Jolie asked.

"Why don't you tell us?"

She crossed her arms over her chest. "There's nothing to tell."

"Start from the beginning."

"But I've already gone through it. Twice." Jolie looked helplessly from one man to the other. "I haven't known Thad very long. We just met. I'm the one who called you. Why are you badgering me?"

Cocking his head to one side, Ross said, "Do you feel as if we're badgering you?"

"Yes."

He smiled knowingly up at Edwards. "What do we always say?"

"Only the guilty feel attacked."

"That's right."

She gasped. "I'm not lying." Oh, God. That was probably something else a guilty person would say, and based on the knowing looks the men gave each other, she'd just confirmed their suspicion.

"Tell us about that ghost town again. What was it Thad said? Something about 'a good place to hide'?"

Jo shook her head. "No. No, *I* said it was a good place to hide a body."

Both men arched a brow in unison.

"Are you insinuating that I'm helping Thad in some way?"

"If there's one thing we know, love makes people do stupid shit."

She shook her head. "You couldn't be more wrong. I'm not helping him. I reported him. And…for the record? I am *not* in love with him." Though her heart did a weird somersault when she said it.

Ross sucked on his teeth. "Go put on something warm, Ms. Duval. We're going on a little field trip and we're leaving in five."

By the time Jo was dressed and ready, Dillon and the agents were out by the pond, two snowmobiles running.

Zak came sprinting out from behind the house, the dogs following close behind, heading straight for them.

"Where you guys going?" he asked Jolie excitedly. "Can I come? I've never been on one of those before." He pointed at the snowmobiles and the men sitting astride one of the sleds wearing heavy parkas and helmets. Even covered up like that, they looked like Feds, not guests.

Simon jogged to catch up to his son. "It's just adults, Zakie. Let's go in and get some hot chocolate."

"Awww…"

Simon tugged him away, and Zak called over his shoulder, "C'mon, Sue!"

Sue had other ideas.

Growling, with the fur standing up at the scruff of her neck, she approached the men slowly, but her growl was drowned out by the rumble of the sleds. When she was only a few feet away, the dog launched herself at the man sitting in front—Jo figured it was Ross because he was shorter—and clamped down on his arm.

The man yelped and Dillon, who was standing between the snowmobiles, jumped into action, grabbing the dog by the scruff and dragging her off.

Agent Ross lifted his visor and scowled. "What the fuck was that?"

"Sorry," Dillon said, holding the snarling dog as it snapped at the agent, seeming even more feral because it was restrained. "It must be the helmets." Dragging her off in the other direction, he called, "I'll put her in the barn before we leave."

Just when Jo was starting to get used to the dog, it became the rabid beast she'd always feared. The attack, coupled with everything else—the Feds, sleeping with a killer, sledding off at dusk to search for said killer—it was all too much.

A wave of dizziness hit her.

She wrapped her arms around her stomach. "I don't feel so good..."

Edwards caught her just as her legs gave out. He lifted his visor and said, "Nice try, lady. But I'm not buying this damsel-in-distress shtick. You know where he is and you're going to help us find him."

He pushed another helmet at her midsection. "Put this on. You'll ride on the other machine with buddy from the ranch."

She snatched the helmet and put it on, fighting the irrational urge to kick the guy as he sat on the sled. Were all FBI agents this arrogant and rude? She'd thought that was just a stereotype. Obviously not.

All she knew was that the agents suspected her of being in cahoots with Thad and it would probably take finding him for them to believe her. So, she'd help them find him.

Suddenly, the gravity of the situation weighed on her and she dropped onto the back of the other snowmobile. What if they never believed her? What if they didn't find Thad or, worse, found him and he turned on her? He could tell them she helped him and then what?

He could mention her journal.

Oh, shit.

She could be charged with aiding and abetting a fugitive.

Seriously, this had to be the absolute worst Christmas holiday Jo had ever had.

THE OLD HOTEL opened up the restaurant for lunch and dinner in the summertime, which meant there were still some canned and dried goods stored in the back of the kitchen. Thad was just in the midst of loading up his backpack when the sound of snowmobile engines echoed between the hills. He couldn't be sure but he figured they were a couple miles off. Maybe more, maybe less.

Joyriders? It could be but Thad knew, he just *knew* it was them coming for him.

Dammit. Now he really wished he'd put a bullet in that badger, because he could be miles away with no tracks if not for that thief. The only thing he had going for him was the cover of darkness, which was almost upon him.

The way he figured it, he had about ten minutes before they got to Silverton. He'd covered his tracks as much as possible but... Thad patted the pocket of his jacket where he'd shoved the broken lock from the door of the hotel. Would they notice this door was missing its lock? Maybe, maybe not, but there was no way to get the lock back in place and hightail it out of town before they arrived. When it came down to a race between a snowmobile and snowshoes, the snowmobile would win every time. Really, there were only two options: have a good old-fashioned shootout or hide.

The problem with a shoot-out was that it would end with either him or someone else taking another bullet. And if he killed that someone else, he'd be a cop killer for real this time.

That left hiding. But where?

Right here.

A voice in his head? Great. Not only had he lost his food, now he was losing his mind.

He nudged an old-fashioned throw rug back from the floor. Underneath was a trapdoor and he was willing to bet that it led to the root cellar. He pulled on the metal ring and lifted, shining his flashlight into the cold, damp space beneath the floor. There was a rickety ladder leading down and a musty smell rising up.

He dropped his snowshoes into the hole and his backpack after them. Then with the flashlight held between his teeth, he descended, making sure that the rug was in place to cover the trapdoor again after it shut. Once down in the cellar, he swept the beam of the flashlight in front of him. Cobwebs hung from wooden rafters and along the dirt walls were ramshackle shelves with a few old milky jars and ancient tin cans.

It's the perfect place to hide a body.

Jolie's voice was a ghost in his ear, making the hair stand up on the back of his neck.

"Let's hope it doesn't come to that, Jolie," he whispered to the silence. "Because I didn't do it and I'm tired of running."

JOLIE NOTICED THE missing lock right away. There was a second—a millisecond maybe—when she considered not mentioning it. But Edwards had been shadowing her the entire time and he must have noticed the missing padlock, since every other door of the old ghost town had one.

"Over here," Edwards called.

How different this was from her last visit, when she'd been dying to peek inside the old buildings and walk around. Now, as she walked across the lobby and through the dining hall of the old hotel, it was like the ghosts were everywhere, flitting between the shadows, making strange sounds from the walls and beneath the floorboards.

"Back here," Ross—who'd gone on ahead—called.

Edwards's flashlight led the way and all four of them congregated in the kitchen storeroom. "He's been here, all right. Look at this."

The shelves had been pilfered, quickly. Cans knocked over, bags ripped open.

"Do you think he's still here?" Edwards asked Ross.

"If he is, he's a fool."

"It was probably a couple days ago," Dillon said.

"How do you figure that?"

"Well, he left on the night of the twenty-eighth or morning of the twenty-ninth. We checked the kitchen and nothing was missing from the house. He doesn't keep much at his place so this is probably the first place he came before heading out into Beaverhead County to avoid people."

"Listen to this guy," Edwards drawled. "Thinking like a real lawman."

Jo glanced at Dillon to see how he responded to the condescending tone of the agent.

Ross ignored his partner. "How far would he have gotten in two days?"

"On snowshoes? He might be twenty, thirty miles away by now. But which direction? Who knows. There's the pass, there's the southern route, northern route..."

Ross tugged on Edwards's sleeve and pulled him in the other direction so they could speak together without Jolie or Dillon hearing. However, their discussion soon turned into an argument, which meant it was loud and clear.

"We go after him now. There's no turning back."

"Are you crazy? With these two? No food, no shelter, no equipment? It's suicide."

"What do you suggest?"

"Why don't you call in some helicopters?" Dillon offered. "There's a lot of back country to cover by snowmobile and pretty hard to track in darkness."

Ross scowled in Dillon's direction, holding up his hand to silence him before lowering his voice so that Jo was unable to hear the rest of the discussion.

"Those guys are not what I expected," Dillon said quietly.

"You mean you didn't expect incompetent assholes," she whispered.

Dillon snickered and then covered it up with a cough as flashlights turned in their direction.

"Okay," Ross said as he rejoined them. "We'll head back to the ranch and start again at first light. He's got to have left some tracks we just have to pray for no snow."

Thank God. Jolie was desperate to get back so that these men could do their job and leave her out of it. Maybe this was her big story but...the truth was, she didn't want it and she didn't want to help these arrogant jerks.

She wanted... Thad.

He lied to you. He used you. He's a killer.

Even now, even after all she'd learned about him and all he'd put her through, she still wanted him. What did that make her? A lunatic? A hopeless romantic? An accomplice to a killer?

Her limbs were numb as she climbed aboard the snowmobile behind Dillon. She shivered for the duration of the ride home as she hugged Dillon's back, and the ride seemed to take three times as long as the way out there. So similar to last time she'd ridden the dogsled back to the ranch, yet so different.

When they finally parked the machines near the shed behind the barn, Edwards took her elbow and escorted her to the lodge, in through the foyer, right to the door of her room.

"What are you doing?" she asked, trying to pull away.

He dragged a chair from her room out into the hall and said, "I'm going to be right here, all night. We'll be leaving at first light, so be ready because you're coming with us."

That didn't make sense. She would just slow them down. Why on earth would FBI agents want her to join them?

Because they don't trust you.

Jo had never been in a situation like this before, where people questioned her integrity. "Fine. I'll be ready." She shut the bedroom door and locked it. Edwards might think he was keeping her in, but she was just as intent on keeping him out. The first thing she did was go into the bathroom and turn on the faucet for a bath, nice and hot. She dumped some of her new bubble bath under the running water, the lavender scent seeming incongruent to her state of mind. But she needed to do something to warm up, to relax, and then she'd try to figure out what to do.

While the tub filled, she went to retrieve her pajamas and saw her cell phone sitting on the desk where she'd left it earlier—before being so rudely interrupted by the Feds. A little meditation music while she soaked the chill out of her bones was just what she needed. However, the second she entered her passcode, she was greeted with over seventeen notifications of messages and three missed calls. She touched the message app.

All were from her brother. All with the same message: call me.

With a glance at the closed door to the hall, Jo went into the bathroom, then shut and locked the door behind her. She hit the redial button and waited. Jacob answered on the first ring.

"Oh, thank God," he said.

"What is it?"

"Tell me the truth. Are you lying to me about Lukas Hunter?"

"No. I swear."

She heard him exhale heavily. "Shit, Jo, I wish you were."

"Why? What's going on?"

"Are you sitting down?" he asked.

"Yes."

"Where are the FBI?"

"One's parked outside my door as we speak. Why?"

"I want you to listen to me very carefully. Those are not FBI agents."

18

Being brave is not doing something worthwhile
in the absence of fear but rather doing something
worthwhile despite fear.

Jo Duval

JO SAT STARING straight ahead, the phone hanging from her
fingertips, the water in the tub coming much too close to
the rim. She reached over and turned off the faucet, pushing her sleeve back in order to fish around in the deep tub
to pull the plug. What the hell was she supposed to do?
Her brother had told her to sit tight and play dumb until
the real authorities arrived. But when would that be? In
an hour? Tomorrow? Thad might not have that long. Who
knew what Ross and Edwards had planned.

Except their names weren't really Ross and Edwards.
They were members of the Salvatori family—a branch of
the family that owned casinos in Atlantic City. It was so
much to take in that for ten minutes, Jo sat there, immobi-
lized. But her stillness did not mean her brain had shut off.
On the contrary. While Jo sat on the toilet seat, her brain
had been working hard, coming up with a plan.

And what she came up with was crazy, partly because
Ms. Internal Editor had fainted from shock and disap-
proval, but even the creative side of her brain knew the
plan was ludicrous. It didn't matter. She was going to go

through with it because she had to, for her sake, for everyone at the ranch and most of all, for Thad.

The first thing she did, once she'd convinced herself to move, was open up her computer and send a message to Gloria and Dillon via their website. They needed to know who these men were and what they intended. She just prayed they'd get the information before it was too late.

Next, she dressed in warm clothes, stuffing as many extra things into her carry-on bag as possible, including the emergency kit she'd picked up at the general store in Half Moon Creek before Christmas. Thank God Edwards hadn't even given her time to take off her boots when he escorted her inside; having no boots would have foiled her plan completely.

Jo turned off her lights and tiptoed to the sliding doors, ever so quietly opening them to slip outside. But no matter how quiet she tried to be, the crunch of the snow beneath her feet sounded extraloud as she made her way across the deck and down the steps. Hiding in the shadows by the side of the house, Jo concentrated on breathing long and deep to calm her racing heart.

It wasn't just sneaking out that had her jittery; it was what she was about to do.

"You can do this, Jo. You can," she muttered beneath her breath, her nerves in desperate need of bolstering.

Making her way across the yard to the barn seemed to take forever, and Jo had to lean against the wall as if she'd run a marathon. She pushed herself away from the wall and jogged around the barn to Thad's bunkhouse. The door was still unlocked and she went in, using the flashlight on her phone to light her way, not willing to take the risk of turning on a light that might be seen from the house.

She found some nonperishables in the cupboards: crackers, jerky, instant soup and candy—black licorice, a whole tinful. That's why he always tasted like licorice. She stuffed the goods in her bag before tiptoeing to Thad's room. This was the critical part. She opened his closet and pulled a shirt out of his laundry basket. Perfect.

Outside, she glanced one way, then the other, watching. Listening. The snowmobiles were still sitting out by the shed, and Jo checked to see if the keys were there. They weren't. That was fine; she didn't plan on taking the machines anyway. They were too loud and she didn't know how to operate one. What she needed was in the shed. After unlatching the lock, she swung the door wide, cringing when the hinges squealed. Thank God—there it was.

Dragging the sled out of the shed wasn't the quietest endeavor either and after shutting the door, she paused to listen.

Only the wind.

Now came the hard part. Jo couldn't do this alone; she needed help. Opening the door to the barn, she whistled softly. "Hey, Sue? You in here?"

All three dogs came scampering up, heads hanging— as if they knew they'd been punished for something—and hind ends wagging, as if in hopes of being forgiven for whatever bad thing they'd done.

Her initial response was to back away, but Jo forced herself to stand still as the dogs milled around her legs. She made herself bend over and scratch each one of them behind the ears and somehow managed to control the urge to turn tail and run. She thought she'd have trouble coercing them to be hitched up to the sled, but she was wrong. The idea of pulling the sled, probably after being cooped up in the barn all day, made the animals ecstatic, and the fact that even Humper sat still as she figured out the harness and tether was a testament to Thad's training of the animals.

Jo clutched her stomach at the thought of him.

"Okay, Jo," she whispered to herself. "No time for histrionics. You've got a job to do."

Now all she had to do was figure out how to drive this thing.

DOGS MIGHT BE TERRIFYING—though these ones weren't as bad as most—but they are smart. She'd give them that. After she let the animals sniff Thad's shirt, it was like Sue knew exactly what Jo wanted her to do. Out in the lead position, Sue simply followed the snowmobile tracks all the way to Silverton and Jo really didn't have to do a thing to steer. Only one problem. When they got to the main street of the old ghost town, the dog kept right on going, barely slowing down to sniff.

Glancing nervously around at the shadows of the abandoned buildings, which seemed larger in the faint moonlight, Jo called, "Hey. You sure you're going the right way?"

It was like the dog understood, turning her head to look at Jo with an exasperated expression before focusing on the task at hand again. Finding her master.

"Okay," Jo said, more to herself than to Sue. "If you say so."

She adjusted her stance on the runners, standing up on the back of the sled the way Thad had done. Standing helped to keep warm, but her legs were starting to stiffen up.

Even though they'd been running for over an hour, Jolie swore the animals picked up the pace. And the reality of what Jo was doing set in. Here she was, Jolie Duval from Chicago—it was the middle of the night, in the middle of winter and she was driving a dogsled.

Mush, mush!

If someone would have told her this a year ago—no, a month ago—she'd have laughed and called them crazy.

Life was weird.

Suddenly the dogs slowed. Sue sniffed one way, and then another, nose to the ground, whining.

"What is it?" Jo stepped stiffly off the runners to approach the dog. The ground beneath her feet was packed down, trampled in fact. Lots of people had come this way at some point.

"Hmm. This doesn't seem right," Jo said. "Where are we?" She got out her phone and turned on the flashlight to sweep the area.

Then she saw the stick, poking up out of the middle of a pile of snow. She knew exactly where she was.

"Oh, Sue. You brought us back to the *quinzee*." She knelt beside the dog. "Thad's not here. He wouldn't—"

The dog jumped up, yipping once before making happy whining noises, her back end going crazy.

Jo stood and turned slowly.

Thad was there, tall as a mountain. A rifle in his hands, aimed at her head.

"WHAT THE HELL are you doing here, Jolie?" Thad demanded, flicking his gaze to the dark trees behind her

"Put the gun down, *Lukas*."

With the gun still propped against his shoulder, he took a step closer and said, "I don't think so."

"We need to talk."

"Where is everyone else?" he growled.

"What do you mean?"

"Don't play dumb. The choppers, the dogs, the Feds?"

"I'm alone."

Convinced she was lying and that agents were using her while hiding somewhere nearby—with sniper rifles ready to do business if he made one wrong move—Thad shook his head.

"What are you going to do, Thad? Shoot me?"

Blowing air through clenched teeth, Thad cautiously lowered the gun. Hell, he wanted to believe she was alone, but he didn't. The problem was, pointing a gun at Jolie was just plain wrong, and he did not want to put her in danger.

Once the gun was down, she came toward him, ripped off her mitten and slapped him soundly across the cheek.

"Ouch," he said out of surprise, not pain. He grabbed her hand before she could hit him again. "I didn't do it, Jolie. I swear to you, whatever those men told you? It's a lie—"

She shut him up by throwing her arms around his neck and kissing him. "I know," she eventually whispered against his mouth. "I know you didn't kill those men."

"Then what the hell are you doing here?"

She shuddered in the circle of his arms, her lips cold against his cheek. She was freezing again. Whatever had possessed this woman to travel by dogsled in the middle of the night he'd find out in a minute, but first he had to get her out of the cold.

"Come on." He took her hand and pulled her toward the snow cave. Switching on the flashlight, he showed her the opening, gave the light to her so she could crawl in first and then crawled in after her. There was enough room inside for two people. Three people would have been a squeeze. Two people and three dogs was a *very* tight squeeze.

"If the dogs are bothering you, I can put them outside. They're used to the cold," he said.

"It's okay." She scratched Sue's head, which was lying on Thad's thigh. "They're good."

"You sure?" he asked as he lit the candle and stuck it into a snow ledge.

"Yes. I'm sure."

Lying beside Jolie on his sleeping bag in the snow structure, Thad gazed in wonder at her in the warm glow of the candlelight. He could not believe it. Never in his wildest dreams had he imagined he'd see Jolie Duval again. In fact, maybe this was a dream. Maybe he'd actually managed to fall asleep because he was so fucking tired, and this was one of those vivid visions of the half dead. Needing to convince himself he wasn't, Thad reached out and stroked her cheek, from brow to chin.

"Thad…" Her lids fluttered closed.

He should not have done that. One word—his name, even though it wasn't the name he was born with—awoke all the cravings for this woman, desires he'd buried. It didn't matter he'd been living rough for days; it didn't matter his life was in jeopardy. All that mattered was that Jolie was here and that she believed him…though for the life of him, he couldn't figure out why.

After drawing a deep breath, he dropped his hand. "Tell me a story, Jolie."

Her eyes opened and a strange look passed over her features. "You read my journal."

"I did."

"You shouldn't have done that."

He angled his head. "No. But I learned a lot." Narrowing his gaze, he said, "What did I do to make you suspect me?"

"You mean the notes in my journal?" She made a derisive sound. "That was a stupid coincidence and I had no idea who you really were until you left."

"But you had my name circled and the website and—"

"It was just a stupid lie I told my brother. I didn't even look at that website until after you'd disappeared." She rubbed a mitten across her face. "The important part is, there are two men staying at the ranch, posing as Feds. But they're not. They're members of the Salvatori family, cousins or something, from Atlantic City."

Rage lanced Thad's gut at the mention of the Salvatori name. He grabbed Jolie's chin, holding her captive. "Are you sure?"

She covered his hand, slid it to her mouth and kissed his palm before gently removing it. "Remember I told you my brother's a DA? Well, he's prosecuted a bunch of cases involving organized crime, so he's got contacts at the FBI. When I told him what was going on, he called them to follow up on your file." Her eyes got a faraway look and one side of her mouth lifted in a soft smile. "He's always looked out for me like that."

He squeezed her hand.

She drew a deep breath. "Anyway, turns out the FBI never received my call. Somehow the Salvatoris hacked the website so that when I called, my number was rerouted to them." Her brows drew together. "I remember now, there was this weird click on the line and it went dead both times I called. Then they called *me* back. I never thought anything of it until now."

"Listen to me, Jolie. If these men are Salvatoris, then they are dangerous and you need to get out of here, right now, because their motto is 'there's only one way to handle a problem—dispose of it.'"

"I know. The authorities are on their way to the ranch right now to pick them up."

"You should have waited there, then. You're not safe with me." He laughed without humor. "Because now I've got the Salvatoris *and* the Feds on my tail."

Jo scooched closer and cupped his face. "No. That's why I had to come, so you wouldn't keep running."

"What are you talking about?"

"The FBI know you didn't do it. They want to find you so that you'll testify *against* the family."

"What?" Thad blinked, desperately wanting to believe her, desperately wanting to stop looking over his shoulder, to stop being on the run for a crime he hadn't committed, but eleven years of discipline could not be broken so easily.

"Those three undercover officers that were shot? One lived."

"No. They all died, I saw them."

"Apparently not. One was in a coma or something, but he woke up a few months later and he told the Feds he saw you being shot. He can't ID the shooters, though. That's where you come in."

Thad stared into Jolie's eyes. Could it be true? Could he have been on the run for nothing? "Why am I still being accused? That doesn't make sense."

"Apparently they've been keeping the officer's information under wraps until they located you, otherwise he'd have been a target."

"Nice," Thad muttered cynically.

Jo rolled closer so that she was lying half on his chest. She stroked the whiskers along his jaw. "You're missing the point. You don't need to run anymore. Tell the Feds what you know and you're a free man."

Jo LET THAD take in the information. It should have been welcome, liberating, but his expression remained stone cold. Maybe after running for so long, it was hard to believe.

His chest rose and fell on a deep breath and when he finally shifted his gaze to her, she said, "Now it's your turn to tell me a story." She gazed down at him in the candlelight. "How the hell did you get embroiled in this mess?"

He didn't answer right away. Instead, he gently eased her off his chest and sat up, reaching for his backpack and taking a journal out of a side pocket. He passed it to her.

"What's this?"

"You gave it to me, remember?"

"I know but…" Jo opened it to find neat and precise handwriting inside. She glanced up, brows arched.

"Fair's fair. I read yours." He used his head to gesture to the book in her hands. "Now you can read mine."

Lying on her stomach to make the most of the candle-light, she flattened the book and began to read.

I met Raina Salvatori at the Pontchartrain Country Club when I worked there in the summer of 2001. It was lust at first sight…

Thad had filled eleven pages in the leather-bound book, chronicling the love affair with Raina Salvatori that resulted in him being asked to "make a hit" in order to be welcomed into the family. She finished the last page slowly, trying to imagine the horror the young Thad—or Lukas—had to endure.

"So, when you wouldn't shoot, they shot you and then took your gun and shot the others?"

"Pretty much."

"Oh, Thad…" She went to touch his face, but he turned away.

"Don't." His lips were compressed and a hard line formed along his jaw. "I deserve the hell I've been in."

"No, you don't."

"Yes, I do, Jolie. I played possum while those cops got killed in cold blood."

"There was nothing you could do."

"Oh, there was plenty I could have done, but did I do

it? Naw. All I did was lie on the ground, pretending to be dead while I listened to three men die." He cringed as if he was picturing it all right now.

"Two men," she corrected.

He shook his head as if the number didn't matter. "I'm a coward, Jolie. A fucking coward."

She tugged his chin toward her. "You were barely more than a kid."

"No excuse. I have replayed that night over and over and there are at least a hundred things I could have done different to save those men. I didn't do one fucking thing."

"You can't beat yourself up about that. It's not that simple."

"You don't know. You weren't there."

"I do know. The characters I write about all do and say these wonderful things, things I wish I could do and say in real life. The only thing is, I *never* say those things because I don't think of them in the moment. I only think of it later, when I'm writing and pretending to be someone else."

"It's not the same," he said, scowling.

"Yes, it is."

Thad exhaled slowly. "Oh, Jolie. I've missed you." He bent down and touched his lips to hers.

"I've missed you, too. So much."

His mouth was soft and gentle, as if he was trying to apologize without words. Maybe even trying to tell her something. What?

Could it be he wanted to tell her that whatever it was she felt for him was reciprocated?

"Jolie." He said her name against her mouth.

"Yes?"

"Oh, Jolie." His mouth continued toward her ear, telling her with hot, sweet breaths what he couldn't say with words.

It was suddenly too warm in the little snow cave and Jolie unzipped her parka, and then unzipped Thad's.

"Whatcha doing, love?"

"I need to touch." She tugged on his shirt tails, pulling them out from his jeans, so that she could slide her hands beneath.

There.

His skin was hot and hard and—oh!—she'd missed him so much. Did his groans mean he'd missed her too?

Carefully, he rolled them over so he was on top. Propped on one hand, he pulled her sweater up, baring her stomach before doing the same to his shirt.

"I need to feel you, skin to skin."

Yes. She needed the same thing, except she had to have his whole chest, flush against her. Only thing was, she couldn't get the buttons on his shirt undone fast enough.

While she worked the buttons, Thad wedged a hand between them, maneuvering beneath the waistband of her tights and panties.

"Thad."

"Oh, sweetheart."

His fingers brushed her clit and Jolie forgot all about the last couple of buttons. Her body arched beneath his, willing his hand deeper, needing a part of his body—even if only his fingers—inside of hers.

Two fingers filled her, pulsing against her inner walls as she clutched at his shoulders. "Yes, Thad. Oh yes."

And then he stopped.

She opened her eyes and lifted her head. "What's wrong?"

"Shh." Thad cocked his head to the side, listening.

Sue started to whine.

"What is it?" she asked.

"Snowmobiles." He looked into her eyes. "We've got company coming and I'm pretty sure it's not the good kind."

19

When traveling, above all trust your gut. It will rarely
lead you astray.

Jo Duval

THAD WAITED IN the trees, his rifle cocked and ready, his
heart pounding hard through his veins. But the gun didn't
waver. He wouldn't let it. Too much was at stake. His life?
Sure. But Jolie's was, too, and there was no way in hell he
was going to let harm come to her. He'd instructed her to
stay inside the snow cave with the dogs. In the dark, unless you knew what to look for, the cave was just a pile of
snow. He'd hidden the sled in the trees and now he waited.

He hadn't realized how he'd actually longed for this moment. Eleven years of waiting. Of knowing it would come
to this, wondering how it would all go down. Preparing.

Unlike when he was a twenty-one-year-old kid, Thad
was a good shot now. He and Curtis practiced shooting tin
cans off fence posts all summer long. He'd shot coyotes,
ravens, skunks and anything else that threatened the live-
stock on the ranch. While he'd never shot a man before,
he wouldn't hesitate to do it if it meant keeping Jolie safe.

And if keeping her safe meant he'd have to take a bullet, he would. No question.

What did that mean? Did he love her? If love was willingly giving up your life for another because you couldn't

bear the thought of any harm coming to that person, then he was wildly in love with Jolie Duval.

The rumble of the snowmobile engines closed in and Thad could make out their headlights flickering through the trees. He consciously slowed his breathing—in for three, out for three—his finger resting lightly on the trigger.

The men drove slowly into the clearing and cut the engines while leaving the headlights on. Stupid. They'd run down the battery in half an hour.

"They're around here somewhere," a tall man said, lifting the visor of his helmet and sweeping the clearing with a flashlight. Thank God the light moved right over the pile of snow.

"Shoot anything that moves," the other said, taking his helmet off and drawing a gun from his jacket.

Well, that confirmed it. These were not the Feds. These were Salvatori's men.

"What's that noise?" The thugs stood still as they listened.

Fuck. One of the dogs—sounded like Sue—was whimpering from inside the snow cave. Thad's finger twitched on the trigger.

"Sounds like dogs." The shorter man pointed to the pile with his gun. "Looks like we found them." He laughed. "Hiding in a fucking pile of snow."

"Let's just blast the shit out of it." The big brute cocked his semiautomatic.

"Easy, Junior. We need to make it look like he killed her, then killed himself."

"Fine. You check it out. I'll cover you."

"You're such a pussy."

"Look at me. I don't like small spaces."

Thad squeezed his eyes shut, took in a deep breath and

reopened them. With the gun snug against his shoulder, he closed his right eye and tilted his head to keep the big man in his sights, his finger slowly tightening.

Wait for it, Thad. Wait...

Someone screamed.

Thad pulled the trigger and the big man went down.

Then all hell broke loose.

Snarling and barking, screaming and cursing. Another shot was fired and one of the dogs cried out in pain. There was too much going on. Snow flying, jaws snapping. The thug rolled in the snow, arms flailing as he fought off an attack from all sides.

Where the hell was Jolie?

Quietly, Thad ran through the trees that made up the perimeter of the clearing. He needed to get to the other side to cover her as she came out.

"Where you think you're going?"

Thad stopped. The big brute stepped out from behind the tree in front of him, his semiautomatic pointed right at him. Even in the darkness, Thad could see the blood staining the guy's jacket.

"Give me your gun, Lukas. Now."

"Why?" Thad needed to stall. Needed to make sure Jo was okay. "You're going to kill us anyway."

"True. But I can make it quick or I can make your girl-friend suffer. Up to you."

"What makes you think she's my girlfriend?" While Thad dropped the gun so that it hung by its strap across his shoulder, his gaze followed the slight movement behind his attacker. Jolie was there; he caught sight of her in the moonlight. What the hell was that in her hand?

Oh, shit.

"Hey, asshole!"

Just as the guy turned, Jolie threw a snowball and it

hit him square in the face. Thad leaped into action. He grabbed the barrel, forcing it skyward while simultaneously kneeing the startled thug in the crotch. With a groan, the man dropped and Thad ripped the gun out of his hands.

From the clearing, another dog whimpered and the sound of boot on flesh alerted him to pending danger. "Jolie, watch out!"

By the snowmobile's headlights, Thad could see the other man staggering toward them, his gun drawn. "You're a dead man, Lukas. But first…" A shot rang out.

"No!"

Thad crashed through the forest and launched himself at the criminal, knocking him to the ground beneath him. His fist connecting with the man's jaw, again and again and again until there was no movement beneath him.

"Jolie? You okay?"

Nothing.

"Jolie!"

"I'm here. I'm fine."

With a sigh of relief, Thad withdrew a roll of duct tape from the inside pocket of his jacket and quickly wound it around the unconscious man's hands and feet, then used his teeth to rip it. Once satisfied, he stood.

He took off in the direction of the snow cave just as he heard the sound of a snowmobile cough to life and then die again.

"Thad! He's trying to get away," Jolie called from off to his left.

He sprinted to where the snowmobiles sat at the edge of the clearing, straight at the big man who sat astride, trying to get the thing started. Thank God he'd chosen the rebuilt Yamaha, because it was touchy once it was flooded. Slowing to a walk and with the man's own gun pointed at him, Thad ordered, "Get up."

"You ain't gonna kill me. If you had it in you, you would have done it already."

"That's true." Thad lowered the barrel.

The guy smirked. "Salvatori was right. You are a pussy."

Aiming at the guy's foot, Thad said, "I may not kill you, but I have no trouble maiming you." He pulled the trigger.

The man screamed and rolled off the sled, clutching at his leg as he writhed in the snow.

Jolie appeared at his side, out of breath. "You okay?"

"Yep."

"Can I help?"

He handed her the tape. "I'll sit on him to keep him still. You tape his hands and feet."

The man was like a rabid animal, biting and cursing as he fought Thad off. But Jolie managed to wind the tape around his hands and feet. When she was done, she made a bow out of duct tape and stuck it to his forehead, like he was a Christmas present.

Thad laughed despite the gravity of the situation. "God, I love you." He took the tape from her and kissed her soundly on the mouth. When he finished, she stared at him with wide-eyed surprise.

From a distance came the welcome sound of a chopper. Thad glanced at the snowmobiles and saw that their headlights were fading.

"Okay," he said to Jolie. "We need to figure out how to signal the chopper." He surveyed the area. "I'm thinking a bonfire is in order."

Jolie gave him an enigmatic smile and said, "That might work for Papa Noel, but I've got my own ideas. Where's the sled?"

Thad led her to where he'd hidden the dogsled in the

trees and Jolie found her bag. From it, she withdrew a large metal kit. She popped it open and withdrew a small red pistol.

"A flare gun?"

"Yessir."

"You are something else, you know that?" Thad kissed her again and then took the gun from her, shooting it off and interrupting the silent night.

"Hey, Thad?"

"Yeah, babe?"

"Where are the dogs?" Jolie asked, a worried expression on her face.

He whistled twice. Digger came loping through the snow, head hanging, tail tucked between his legs. "Hey, buddy. Where's your mama?" He whistled again and Humper appeared, walking slowly and whimpering.

No sign of Sue.

"I'll check over here, you check over there," Jolie said, pointing.

Thad started toward the *quinzee*, whistling and calling, a sick feeling scratching at the pit of his stomach.

"Thad!"

He ran toward her voice, finding her back toward the trees, sitting in the snow with Sue's head in her lap. Jo looked up as he approached, tears coursing down her cheeks. "Oh, Thad. I'm so sorry. She was shot. This damn dog took a bullet to save my life."

JOLIE HAD BEEN up for how many hours straight? She tried to count but her mind was too muddled because she was so tired. They'd gotten back to the ranch in the wee hours of the morning. Then they'd spent the better part of the day being interviewed by the FBI—the real FBI this time—and now she'd finally been released. Even though most of the guests had booked to stay longer, the Feds had insisted everyone who wasn't involved in *the incident* go home, so Jolie never had a chance to say goodbye to Kaylee and Evan or Zak and Simon.

She'd have to get their contact info from Gloria, because, after all they'd shared and been through, they were family now.

Stumbling into her bedroom, Jolie collapsed onto the bed. She'd lie down just for a couple of minutes, that's all, because she wanted to be there when Thad was done with his questioning.

However, when she woke up, her room was dark and for a second, she had no idea where she was. A thud from outside her French doors brought her to her feet. She drew back the blinds just as another snowball hit the glass.

She slid open the doors to find Thad sitting in the hot tub wearing a grin.

She pulled on her wool socks and padded across the deck. "Not a bad arm," she said. "For a Most Wanted man."

"Not anymore, I'm not."

She sat on the edge of the hot tub. "Sure you are. You're on *my* Most Wanted list."

"Is that so?"

"Maybe."

"Well now, why don't you take off all those bulky clothes and show me what you mean by that statement?"

She laughed. "Aren't you tired?"

"Naw, plenty of time to sleep when I'm dead." He tugged on the hem of her sweater, snaking a wet hand up underneath.

She slapped his hand away. "That's not funny, considering everything you've been through."

"Everything *we've* been through." He grabbed a handful

of sweater again. "Now, you going join me in this soaker or am I going to have to pull you in, clothes and all?"

"I'm not wearing a bathing suit."

"I seem to recall that not being a problem in the past."

"Yes, but…" After glancing over her shoulder, Jo pulled her sweater over her head. "That was before there were federal agents milling about. After the last forty-eight hours, I don't feel like being charged now with lewd behavior." She paused, resting her hands on the band of her leggings.

"Ah, but the Jolie I know and love thrives on living on the edge, so…" Thad leaned out of the tub, offering to help pull down her tights.

"Did I just hear correctly?" She turned her back to him and shimmied the snug material down her legs. "Did you just tell me you loved me?"

"Don't take it too seriously. I say that to all the women who save my life."

"Must be hundreds of them." She peeked over her shoulder and was rewarded by a lovely groan from Thad. Turning her back, she unclasped her bra and let it fall to the ground, then she inched her panties over her hips and down her legs.

"Heaven have mercy," Thad whispered. "You need to get in this tub right now."

Jo climbed the steps and slid swiftly beneath the water. She didn't even get a chance to sit before Thad pulled her onto his lap, a warm hand cupping her head, drawing her close for a kiss. His lips were hot and wet and soft. When she pulled away, the playfulness was gone and she touched the lines beside his eyes. "You are tired."

"I don't care," he said raggedly. "The truth is, Jolie, I'd be a dead man if not for you."

She nuzzled her head into the lovely crook between chin

and shoulder. "I saved your life, you saved mine. We're even." She breathed in the scent of his damp flesh.

"I didn't save your life, Sue did."

Jolie stroked Thad's chest. "I'm so sorry about Sue."

"Didn't you hear?"

"Hear what?"

"She's going to make it. Her leg was shattered and irreparable, so they had to take it off. Poor thing'll be a tripod dog, but she's alive." He looked away as his jaw tensed and air hitched in his throat. "I'm sorry," he said a moment later. "I know she's just a damned dog."

"She's not just a damned dog. She's the best dog. Ever."

Thad held both sides of her face when he kissed her this time. Against her lips, he whispered, "I don't need to run anymore, Jolie."

"I know." She licked at the seam of his mouth, nuzzling against him.

"I don't need to hide. Not from the authorities…" He took a deep breath. "And not from you."

She nibbled his chin.

"And when a man gets a second chance in life—" he paused to pull back so he could look at her "—he doesn't want to waste one second of it."

She wriggled in his lap, rubbing his erection between her legs. But Thad took hold of her hips and held her still. "Before you kill me by doing that, I need to ask you something."

"What?" She caressed the lovely muscles of his shoulders that peeked above the water level.

"I know it's sudden and I know we haven't known each other very long, but—"

"But…?"

"See, I don't ever want you out of my sight again. I know it's crazy, it's just, I've never—"

She touched his face, feeling an overwhelming connection to this man. "It's the same for me."

"Is it?"

She nodded. "I've never met anyone like you. I love being with you. But more important, I like the person I am when we're together. I like her a lot."

"I like her, too." Thad ran his thumb across her bottom lip. "I more than like her." He descended, groaning into her mouth as his lips slanted across hers, his tongue sweeping inside, searching for something with a desperation Jolie wasn't used to but that she somehow understood.

"Where do we go from here, Jolie? I don't know what the future holds."

"I think we figure it out as we go. This is new, for both us, and…"

A pop followed by a whistling sound split the night. Then there was an echoing bang that sounded like a gunshot.

"What the hell?"

"Look," Jolie said, pointing to the colorful sky to the north. "Fireworks." She laughed. "Oh, my God. It's New Year's Eve."

Jolie sat snuggled on Thad's lap, her head tucked beneath his chin, his arms around her waist holding her close while they watched the fireworks display that must have been set off from a neighboring property.

"Happy New Year, Thad." She turned to gaze up at him. "Happy New Life."

"Right back at you, Jolie Duval."

She settled herself comfortably against his chest. "I do love fireworks," she said with a contented sigh.

"You want fireworks?" He kissed her neck while his hands slid from her waist to her thighs. "I'll give you fireworks." He turned her in his lap so that he could kiss her mouth. "Sha, I'll give you more than fireworks. I aim to give you whatever you want."

"All I want is you, Thad. That's it." She let him kiss her before she pulled away again. "Oh, and I want permission to write your story. I hope that's okay."

"I'd be honored." He cupped her cheek. "You going to include all the good juicy bits between you and me?"

"No," she said, "I think I'll keep that just between us. But..."

"But what?"

"But I think I need more material. So..." Jolie had to bite her lip to keep her smile in check. In a husky voice, she said, "Tell me, Thaddeus Knight, you said you're a hand. What does that mean, exactly?"

At first Thad frowned and then it was like a light came on as he remembered the entry in her journal. "I could tell you," he said slowly. "But showing you would be way more fun." His hands fondled her beneath the surface of the water.

She arched into him. "Then you'd better show me."

"Oh, Jolie. It'd be my pleasure."

* * * * *

*Watch for the next Harlequin Blaze
from Daire St. Denis, WILD SEDUCTION,
available April 2017.*